W9-CFL-973

***"I'll share my fish with you if you'll cook them,"* Thorn said.**

"Are you inviting yourself to dinner?" Rachel shook her head in exasperation. "Did anyone ever tell you you're a pushy person?"

"Once or twice. Now, if I don't catch anything, I'll pick up steaks for our dinner."

Rachel sighed. "I've lived in Iowa long enough to know there isn't anything that can be done about a tornado except to ride it out."

"Is that what you're going to do, ride out this weekend?" he asked.

"Either that, or hide under a table until it blows over and you leave."

In a gesture that surprised them both, Thorn reached out and stroked the soft skin of her throat with the back of his knuckles. "It's liable to be a rough ride. The way you make me feel isn't calm."

Spirals of searing heat rushed through her. "Thorn—"

His mouth covered hers with an immediate hunger, and she was unable, unwilling to resist him. . . .

WHAT ARE *LOVESWEPT* ROMANCES?

They are stories of true romance and touching emotion. We believe those two very important ingredients are constants in our highly sensual and very believable stories in the *LOVESWEPT* line. Our goal is to give you, the reader, stories of consistently high quality that may sometimes make you laugh, sometimes make you cry, but are always fresh and creative and contain many delightful surprises within their pages.

Most romance fans read an enormous number of books. Those they truly love, they keep. Others may be traded with friends and soon forgotten. We hope that each *LOVESWEPT* romance will be a treasure—a "keeper." We will always try to publish

LOVE STORIES YOU'LL NEVER FORGET
BY AUTHORS YOU'LL ALWAYS REMEMBER

The Editors

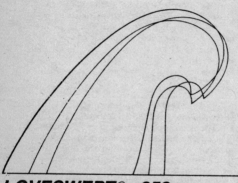

LOVESWEPT® • 352

Patt Bucheister
Elusive Gypsy

BANTAM BOOKS
NEW YORK • TORONTO • LONDON • SYDNEY • AUCKLAND

ELUSIVE GYPSY
A Bantam Book / September 1989

LOVESWEPT® and the wave device are registered
trademarks of Bantam Books, a division of
Bantam Doubleday Dell Publishing Group, Inc.
Registered in U.S. Patent
and Trademark Office and elsewhere.

All rights reserved.
Copyright © 1989 by Patt Bucheister.
Cover art copyright © 1989 by Garin Baker.
No part of this book may be reproduced or transmitted
in any form or by any means, electronic or mechanical,
including photocopying, recording, or by any information
storage and retrieval system, without permission in
writing from the publisher.
For information address: Bantam Books.

If you would be interested in receiving protective vinyl
covers for your Loveswept books, please write to this address
for information:

Loveswept
Bantam Books
P.O. Box 985
Hicksville, NY 11802

ISBN 0-553-22029-2

Published simultaneously in the United States and Canada

Bantam Books are published by Bantam Books, a division
of Bantam Doubleday Dell Publishing Group, Inc. Its trademark, consisting of the words "Bantam Books" and the
portrayal of a rooster, is Registered in U.S. Patent and
Trademark Office and in other countries. Marca Registrada.
Bantam Books, 666 Fifth Avenue, New York, New York 10103.

PRINTED IN THE UNITED STATES OF AMERICA

O   0 9 8 7 6 5 4 3 2 1

One

It was a rotten shame. His gray-haired seventy-two-year-old great-aunt had lost her sweet little mind. There was no other explanation. No matter how many times Dr. Thorn Cannon read the postcard he'd received that morning, he came up with the same conclusion. His aunt had flipped.

WON LOTTERY IN FLORIDA. MARRIED TAYLOR
MEAD ON SATURDAY. LOVE, AUNT EDITH.

Turning the card over, he scowled at the photo of palm trees silhouetted against a colorful sunset. The postmark was dated four days earlier, Waikiki, Hawaii.

Tossing the postcard onto his desk, he recalled the last time he had talked with his aunt. She had been excited about an upcoming trip to Florida with a senior citizens tour group. Apparently her little junket had been chock-full of unscheduled surprises.

Instead of coming back with several rolls of film and some tacky souvenirs, she absconded to Hawaii with a man and millions. And sent her only nephew a lousy postcard.

Since his partner had been on vacation the previous week, Thorn had been exceptionally busy taking care of Richard's patients as well as his own. However, he hadn't been so preoccupied, he would have noticed receiving a message that Edith had called to invite him to her wedding. Obviously, she thought the postcard was adequate notice. It wasn't.

After receiving the card, he had phoned his aunt's neighbor, Mr. Grundy. He had informed Thorn his aunt wasn't home, which Thorn had already figured out for himself. The elderly neighbor had told him she had come home for a few days after the trip to Florida, gotten married, and left for Hawaii the next day on her honeymoon.

When Thorn asked who might know where his aunt was staying in Hawaii, Mr. Grundy mumbled, "The justice of the peace," before he hung up.

Thorn simply couldn't believe his aunt would get married without asking him to the wedding, or at least telling him beforehand that she was getting married. He was the only family Edith Warwick had. He had always thought he and his aunt had a close relationship. Certainly close enough to be invited to her wedding. Granted, he hadn't been able to get to Bowersville to see her very often during the last three years, but he had contacted her by phone every few weeks to make sure she was all right.

Six months earlier she had spent several days in Des Moines with him, and had allowed him to arrange for a complete physical for her. Chronologically she was seventy-two, but she had the spirit of a woman much younger. She had been like a whirlwind, breezing in and out of his apartment and his clinic, leaving smiles in her wake as she swept by. From years of experience, Thorn knew she didn't understand the meaning of the word moderation. Everything she did, she did with enthusiasm and contagious excitement, without any thought or consideration for herself.

As a physician he was concerned for her health. As her nephew he was just plain worried about her.

As he sat behind his desk in his office, he reread the postcard although he knew what it said by heart. He was going to have to go to Bowersville. He needed to find out who Taylor Mead was, if his aunt had actually gotten married, and whether or not she was in her right mind. Luckily it was his partner's weekend to be on call for emergencies, so Thorn would be free to leave Des Moines.

It took him an hour to finish seeing his patients and to go over a few charts with his partner. Fridays were always scheduled lighter than the rest of the week, and he was able to leave earlier than normal. He stopped by his apartment to pack enough clothes for the weekend. It was late afternoon by the time he threw his small leather suitcase in the trunk of his silver-gray BMW and got behind the wheel. Because of an emergency call, he hadn't had much sleep the previous night, but that didn't stop him from making the trip. If the distance had been longer, he probably would have settled for a good night's rest before driving to the small town. He was impatient but not stupid.

As he drove he felt the tension in his shoulders

and forced himself to relax. He took a deep breath and wondered what in hell was wrong with him. It was a question that had popped into his mind a number of times during the last couple of months. An odd restlessness had made him unusually edgy, a trait foreign to his normal easygoing nature. Maybe Richard was right. He needed a vacation. Actually his partner had been more specific. What he needed, according to Richard, was to spend a shameless week somewhere with a shameless woman. Even if it didn't get rid of his case of the fidgets, it would undoubtedly do a lot for his libido.

The two-hour drive went quickly. The last twenty miles were on a two-lane road where he met only three other vehicles, one a tractor plodding slowly along on the narrow road. The tires of his car rolled roughly over the railroad ties that passed as a bridge spanning the dam on the Little Sioux River, and he entered the town of Bowersville, Iowa.

As he slowly drove past the grain elevator and the gas station on the left side of River Road, which comprised the one-block main street, Thorn felt as though he had stepped back in time. Nothing ever seemed to change in Bowersville. It was as though clocks ticked slower in the quiet town.

Bowersville was a tiny town of five hundred people, give or take a few. There were more residents in the local graveyard than there were in the homes and farms situated in and around the town proper. The small community had remained virtually unchanged since he was a child and would spend several weeks every summer in his aunt's rambling old Victorian house. The pace was slow and sedate, which was the way the townspeople preferred it. The children rode a bus to a consolidated school situated between Bowersville and Algona. There was no police force, hospital, or movie theater. There were two small churches almost as old as the town itself.

Nine buildings were ranked along the west side of the main street. Only one building stood across from them, a tidy brick one that housed the post office, utilities and phone companies, and held the city records.

The hardware store had snow shovels stacked in front of it, although it was a warm September day. Thorn wouldn't have been surprised if they were left there year-round. The advertisements stuck into the windows of the drugstore were faded from sunlight and time. Peabody's Sundries served as the only grocery store, offering a variety of basics but skimpy on gourmet items. Next to Peabody's was a dry goods store. A sign on the door of Ruby's Café offered a five-cent cup of coffee, which was an indication of how long the restaurant had been in business. The windows and doorways of three buildings farther down were boarded up. At the end of the line of businesses was the bane of the women in the town for the past fifty years—Floyd's Pool Hall.

As in most small communities, everyone in Bowersville tended to know each other's affairs. But Thorn couldn't think of a single person to call or see in order to get more information about his aunt other than Mr. Grundy. The man hadn't exactly been a fount of information over the telephone, but perhaps in person Thorn would be able to get some better answers. One person in particular he wanted to talk to was the justice of the peace, the man who had married his aunt to some stranger.

On impulse Thorn parked in front of Ruby's Café and got out. The original Ruby had long since passed away. Ruby's granddaughter, Mrs. Lindstrom, flipped hamburgers, poured coffee, and gathered the news about everything that went on in and around town as well as Ruby had. He was going to start with her.

He wasn't disappointed. Mrs. Lindstrom did indeed know about Edith Warwick winning the lottery and suddenly marrying. She had been there along with half the town when the justice of the peace had offically married Edith and Taylor Mead in Edith's home. While pouring Thorn a cup of coffee and placing a slice of freshly baked apple pie on the counter in front of him even though he hadn't ordered it, she described the entire ceremony, from what Edith wore to how distinguished Edith's new husband was.

Lowering her voice, she added in a conspiratorial whisper, "Mr. Mead is a little younger than Edith, you know."

Visions of a sleazy gigolo flashed through his mind. "Exactly how young is he?"

The plump woman shrugged. "Who can tell these days? Just younger." Then she proceeded to tell him about her bunions. She knew Edith Warwick Mead's nephew was a doctor and wasn't about to let an opportunity for some free medical advice slip by.

Thorn only partly heard the woman's complaints. He was more concerned than ever about his aunt. And angry. What was the justice of the peace thinking of, marrying a seventy-two-year-old woman to a younger man she had just met? It was one of the first questions he was going to ask the doddering old fool who had done exactly that.

Mrs. Lindstrom greeted another customer and automatically poured the man a cup of coffee. After chatting with him for a few minutes, she walked around the small café to refill the other customers' cups.

When she got back to Thorn, he shook his head as she was about to pour him more coffee. "No, thanks. I'd like to talk to the justice of the peace who married my aunt, Mrs. Lindstrom. Would you know where—"

"Gone fishin'," said a man who had just come in. "Bought bait from me about an hour ago."

A discourse began between the man, Mrs. Lindstrom, and several other patrons about the best fishing spots on the Little Sioux River. All agreed it was a bit late in the year to have much success, although some catfish were still biting once in a while on warm days like this one.

Thorn wasn't interested in hearing fish stories. He tossed some cash onto the counter near his uneaten pie and left the café. He figured the justice of the peace wouldn't be that hard to find. Having spent many summers with his aunt, he was familiar with the Little Sioux River and the best fishing spots. He was going to wring some information out of the old fool before he tossed him into the river.

Tired, frustrated, irritated, and worried, Thorn knew it wasn't the best time to confront the man who had officiated at her wedding. But he was going to anyway.

He drove back toward the river and parked off the road near a well-worn path beside the bridge. It was as good a place as any to start the search. For fifteen minutes he walked along the shore without seeing a single soul along either bank of the river. He was about to turn back when he heard the sound of splashing on the other side of some bushes and trees.

Either a fisherman had caught a whopper of a fish or had fallen into the river. He shoved back a branch of the maple tree barring his way and stepped through the bushes. The riverbank was high, barring his view of the water from where he stood. On the grass several feet away was an ancient fishing creel, a bamboo pole complete with red and white bobber and hook, and a small round cardboard container that had tiny holes poked into its lid. On top of a fallen log he saw a folded towel next to a pile of clothing. There was a pair of faded jeans, a white shirt, and moccasins small enough to fit a boy.

And a pair of ice-blue lace-trimmed panties.

It was the last item of apparel that slowed Thorn's step as he walked toward the edge of the river.

An amused female voice came from the slow-moving water. "I don't recommend you come any closer. The bank is slippery."

Thorn stopped and stared. A vision of startling beauty appeared in the river in front of him. Dark green water swirled around the bare shoulders of a stunning woman. Sunlight glittered on the surface of the water, as though she were surrounded by floating diamonds. Her light brown hair had been twisted and gathered casually on top of her head, several curls cascading over her ears and clinging damply to her slender shoulders. The soft upper swell of her breasts rose out of the water, glistening with moisture. He silently cursed the dark water for obstructing the rest of her from his view although his imagination was working overtime to fill in the fantasy.

And she had to be a fantasy. It was the only explanation for the strange effect the sight of her was having on him.

Glints of gold highlighted her dark brown eyes as she met his gaze calmly. Her lips were parted slightly, drawing his attention to them. He became fascinated with her mouth, wondering how her lips would taste, how her tongue would feel rubbing against his.

"I came looking for the justice of the peace," he said abstractedly, "and found a mermaid."

When she smiled he felt an odd jolt and had to force himself to concentrate on what she was saying. His gaze remained fixed on her mouth. "There are," she said, "two reasons people usually want a justice of the peace, to be married or to have something notarized. Which are you?"

"Neither."

"Good," she said with lazy satisfaction. "As you can see, I'm not exactly dressed to perform a ceremony, and I don't have my notary seal with me."

Thorn stared. "You're the justice of the peace?"

"I am *a* justice of the peace. At the moment, a very wet justice of the peace."

"I noticed. Also a very naked justice of the peace," he drawled.

"I couldn't resist taking one last swim," she replied. "There won't be many more days like this before the weather changes."

Leaning a shoulder against a tree, he crossed his arms over his chest and asked lazily, "You don't like bathing suits?"

She swept a handful of water into her palm and ran her hand over her other arm, slowly and sensually, relishing the feel of the cool water. The sun caught the glittering drops of moisture on her lightly tanned skin. Her eyes closed with pleasure. "It's not the same," she murmured.

"I can see that," he said softly, his gaze skimming over her. Jealous. He was jealous of the water flowing over her. It should be his hands instead.

Hearing the change in the tone of his voice, Rachel Hyatt opened her eyes and met the man's penetrating gaze. Her voice was cooler, with a hint of mockery. "I imagine you can see a great deal since you haven't stopped staring at me. Would you throw me that towel over there, please?"

"Why?"

She smiled faintly. "I could give you a number of reasons. The main one is I'd like to get out of the water."

"Don't let me stop you."

Rachel studied him, his slight smile and the gleam of humor and sensuality in his eyes. The framed photos Edith had in her home of Thorn Cannon didn't do him justice. He was taller than she had expected, possibly three or four inches above her own five feet ten. His hair was as dark as obsidian, his eyes a rich deep blue. The photos hadn't shown the intensity in his gaze, the sensual grace in the way he moved. Even standing still as he was now, he emanated confidence, authority . . . and a potent sexuality.

He also looked exhausted. She became aware of the tired lines at the corners of his mouth and around his eyes. She wondered if they were caused by work or by late nights spent out on the town. Since he was Edith's favorite topic of conversation, Rachel knew he was in his early thirties and had a medical practice in Des Moines. What Edith failed to mention was how compellingly male he was. When he looked at her, she felt an unsettling awareness covering her like a too-warm blanket.

She wasn't sure she liked the sensation. No, she corrected herself. The problem was she did like it. Too much. His gaze seemed to stroke her, making her feel as though a current of electricity ran from him to her.

Knowing she was at a disadvantage under the circumstances, she said succinctly, "The towel."

Thorn walked over to the log and picked up the towel. Then he tossed it to her.

Holding the towel in front of her, she waded into the shallow water, then wrapped the towel around her, tucking in one corner beside her left breast. The long length of her legs were exposed since the material ended at the tops of her thighs.

Mesmerized by the sight of her scantily-clad body, Thorn stood rooted to the ground. For a moment it seemed as though she would never stop rising out of the water. She was taller than most women he knew, making him wonder how well they would fit together.

As she stepped out of the river, her foot slipped on the muddy bank. He quickly closed the distance between them and reached for the hand she had flung out to balance herself. His fingers closed around hers, and he pulled her up onto the grassy bank.

Once she was on more solid ground, she expected him to release her hand. He didn't, and she looked up at him.

He was staring at her as though he had never seen a woman before. She saw his gaze slide upward from her bare feet over her thighs, her hips, to her breasts. It wasn't the first time she'd been ogled by a man, but the way Thorn looked at her made her feel oddly vulnerable and exposed—and not just physically.

She pulled her hand free. "Are you going to tell me why you've come to Bowersville, Dr. Cannon, or are you just going to stand there and stare at me?"

She knew who he was, Thorn thought. That shocked him. But not as much as the absurd feeling he should know who she was. Deep within him, a part of him recognized her although he had never seen her before.

Feeling as though his mind had been nudged over a cliff, he asked, "How do you know who I am?"

"Your aunt has photos of you everywhere in her house."

"You have me at a disadvantage. I know you're the justice of the peace, but I don't know your name."

"Rachel Hyatt." She paused but didn't see any recognition of her name in his eyes. "Since you don't remember me, I guess you also don't recall putting a frog down my sweater when I was six years old."

His disbelief was evident in his face. He stepped back to see her more clearly. "I did what?"

"I was waiting outside Peabody's for my grandfather, and you came along with a string of fish. You also had a frog in your pocket you wanted to show to me. Then you put it down the front of my sweater. You were disappointed when I didn't scream. I removed the frog and gave it back to you."

He gazed at her with astonishment. "I don't remember you." He couldn't imagine ever forgetting someone like her. "Rachel Hyatt," he murmured, as though saying her name would jog his memory. "Rachel Hyatt."

"In the flesh," she said flippantly.

It was a poor choice of words. He was having a hard enough time trying not to think about her magnificent body skimpily covered by the towel. "You've obviously changed."

She shrugged. "People do. I don't imagine you run around putting frogs down girls' sweaters anymore either."

A slow smile curved his mouth. "I gave that up a couple of years ago."

He raised his hand to touch her. There wasn't anything he wanted more. Gently brushing a damp tendril of hair away from her cheek, he let his finger remain on her moist skin.

She stiffened under his touch. "I don't imagine it would be a good trait for a physician to have," she said, faintly alarmed to hear a huskiness in her voice.

He was disconcerted to realize it didn't seem to bother her to be practically naked in front of him, but she didn't want him to touch her. He was finding it amazingly difficult to articulate reasonable questions when his attention kept wandering to the knot holding the towel in place. Feeling the need to put some distance between them, he dropped his hand and stepped back. It was either move away from her or pull her down onto the grassy bank and strip away the towel.

"Is it true you performed the wedding ceremony between my aunt and some strange man?"

"He isn't strange to her."

Anger and frustration hardened his voice. "Doesn't it bother your conscience even one little bit that you were responsible for marrying a seventy-two-year-old woman to some guy she had only just met?"

She tilted her head to one side and countered his question with one of her own. "Why does it bother you so much that Edith has gotten married? Her age? Or the fact that she's suddenly a wealthy woman?"

Thorn didn't know whether to strangle her or shove her onto her back and make love to her. Both needs were strong within him, even though they contradicted each other.

"When you get to know me better," he said, his voice quietly controlled, "you'll realize that was a stupid remark."

"Since I won't be getting to know you, I'll never know if I've made a stupid remark or not, will I?"

"I need some answers, and I'm not leaving until I get them. I'm deeply concerned about my aunt."

Rachel walked over to the log and reached for her shirt. "Your aunt is fine, Dr. Cannon. I've never seen her happier." She slid her arms into the sleeves and buttoned up the front, leaving the top few buttons undone. "Edith is the happiest woman I've ever known. She always has been. It didn't take winning the lottery or getting married to do that."

Thorn watched in fascination as the towel slowly slid to the ground. The tail of her shirt brushed her upper thighs, provocatively but adequately covering her. She was incredibly tall and deliciously sexy, a combination that held him enthralled. He realized he was irrationally angry that she appeared to be perfectly at ease dressing in front of him.

"Do you do this sort of thing often?" he asked.

"Do what?"

"Dress in front of strange men."

Her smile could make a man weak when he needed to be strong. "In what ways are you strange?"

Dragging his mind back to the subject of his aunt, he ignored her question and asked one of his own. "How did Edith meet this guy?"

She picked up her panties and gracefully tugged them on. It wasn't the first time Rachel had gotten dressed with a minimum of clothing to guard her privacy. As a model, she had quickly lost her sense of modesty when swift changes had been the norm rather than the exception.

For some reason, though, the way this man looked at her made her feel exposed, as though he could see more than mere flesh. His blatant staring disturbed her. He disturbed her.

In response to his question, she asked, "You knew about the tour she took to Florida?"

He nodded, his gaze reluctantly leaving her long, tanned legs.

"While she was there, she bought a single lottery ticket and ended up winning eleven million dollars. One of the other members of the tour was a retired banker, Taylor Mead, who offered to advise her about how to invest her new wealth."

Thorn frowned. "I bet he did. And decided to cut himself in for a large chunk by sweeping her off her feet."

"If anyone was doing the sweeping, it was Edith. If you had seen them together, you would have known that they genuinely care about each other. They share the same sense of humor, like the same things, and enjoy each other's company."

She picked up her jeans and pulled them on. Aware he was watching her every move, she took a narrow belt and fastened it loosely around her waist over the shirt. As she slipped her feet into scruffy moccasins, she reached up and took the clasp out of her hair. Long brown curls laced with blond streaks collapsed on her shoulders in a mass.

The clothing didn't make any difference, Rachel realized. He was still watching her intently. "What are you doing here, Dr. Cannon?" she asked bluntly.

Thorn could barely make sense of her question. Knowing she wasn't wearing a bra was provoking his hormones and shifting his imagination into overdrive.

"I told you. I'm concerned about Aunt Edith."

"Don't you think she's old enough to take care of herself?"

He ran his hand through his dark hair in an abstracted gesture. "All I got was a postcard from her saying she won the lottery and that she's married. No phone call. No invitation to the wedding. I find it hard to believe she would get married and not even tell me or invite me to the wedding. It all seems so fast and furtive, as though she had something to hide. I came down here to find out what's been going on."

"Maybe she knew you would disapprove."

Thorn studied her expression carefully. He hadn't heard criticism in her voice and now looked for it in her eyes. "I don't disapprove, Rachel." It was the first time he'd used her name, and he liked the feel of it on his tongue. "I just want to understand what's going on with my aunt, to make sure she's all right and hasn't done anything dangerous or stupid."

She returned his gaze without comment.

Rachel Hyatt was a puzzle to him. She wore an expensive perfume, and old faded jeans over sexy underclothing. She was staggeringly beautiful but let her words make an impression rather than her looks. Even in casual clothing there was a sophistication and elegance in the way she carried herself, an understated grace that attracted him. It was irritating to realize she didn't appear equally impressed with him.

"What in hell are you doing here?" he asked softly.

She blinked at the quiet vehemence in his voice. "I told you. I couldn't resist going for a swim."

He shook his head. "I mean here in Bowersville."

"I've often asked myself the same question," she answered with faint irony. "The easiest answer is it seemed like a good idea at the time. When my grandfather died, he left everything to me. It turned out to be more than I expected."

"You don't belong here," he said baldly. "I can picture you in New York wearing designer clothes, going to expensive restaurants, and eating off fine china. You're much too sophisticated for this little town."

Rachel looked away. He had unintentionally hit a nerve. He was right. She didn't belong in Bowersville. But she didn't belong in New York either. She didn't know where she belonged. Well, it was her problem and had nothing to do with him.

Lifting her chin defiantly, she brought her gaze

back to his. "We were talking about your aunt, not me."

His eyes narrowed at the coolness in her voice. She had a valid point. He had come to Bowersville to learn more about his aunt's marriage. That was all. But that was before he had met Rachel Hyatt.

"I have to admit to being curious about why my sainted aunt has gone off half-cocked with some fortune hunter. I'd like to know why she has suddenly married a man she's known only a short time." His voice hardened. "She's seventy-two years old, for heaven's sake."

"There's no age limit in trying to find happiness, Dr. Cannon."

"You married them. Can you guarantee that's what she's found?"

"I performed a legal ceremony, not a miracle. As a member of the medical profession, you should know better than anyone that life doesn't come with guarantees. Edith has found someone to care for and who cares about her. As to the speed of their marriage and the trip to Hawaii, I don't imagine at their age they want to waste much time."

"Mrs. Lindstrom at the café said this Taylor Mead is younger than my aunt. Can you blame me for being suspicious about the man being after her money?"

Suddenly Rachel smiled, her eyes glittering with amusement. "On the marriage license Taylor Mead had put down his age as seventy. He's two years younger than Edith, hardly a teenager."

Thorn was silent for a long moment. Everything she had said made sense, and maybe down deep he knew it did. The one puzzling fact he couldn't put aside was that his aunt hadn't tried to contact him about such an important event in her life. Was there something she didn't want him to know?

Watching Thorn, Rachel felt a part of her respond to him. He seemed oddly confused and vulnerable, emotions she doubted were ones he experienced often. When he had watched her leave the river, he had worn self-confidence like a cloak. Why did she feel he needed some sort of reassurance about his aunt? Perhaps it was because of the vulnerability she sensed within him that made her offer a suggestion.

"Edith is supposed to phone me tomorrow night from Hawaii. I could ask her to call you at your home in Des Moines if you like."

Without being aware he had made the decision, Thorn heard himself say, "I'm staying the weekend in Bowersville."

"There aren't any hotels in Bowersville," she said quickly, feeling threatened without knowing why.

"I'll stay at my aunt's house."

With a sense of inevitability, she gathered up her fishing gear and the towel. "You'll have to follow me home then. I have the key to her house."

Thorn noticed how her jeans hugged her thighs and bottom as she bent over. She might not be thrilled he would be sticking around for a couple of days, but he was beginning to look forward to the weekend for reasons other than the opportunity to talk with his aunt.

Her car had been parked on the other side of the road behind some bushes, which was why he hadn't seen it earlier. When he saw she drove a flashy red

Porsche, he wasn't even surprised. The events of this day had saturated his capacity for the unexpected.

Or so he thought.

Following her car, he drove along River Road and up the hill, turning when she did into a long drive-way. He parked behind her car and stared at the rather shabby colonial-style house, its paint faded and a few shutters broken. It wasn't the type of home he expected her to live in.

By the time he got out of his car, Rachel was on the porch unlocking the front door. As he approached, she said over her shoulder, "I'll be back in a minute with the key."

The lack of an invitation didn't stop him from entering the house. He wasn't going to be shut out that easily, literally or figuratively. Rachel was no-where in sight. In fact, there was nothing in sight. The foyer was empty. Completely empty. There were no rugs, no tables, no plants, nothing. Walking far-ther inside, he glanced into the living room. It, too, was devoid of furniture. The floor was bare wood, the windows curtainless.

He looked up when he heard soft footsteps on the stairs. Rachel paused halfway down the steps when she saw him standing in the foyer. She hadn't ex-pected him to come into the house. Damn him, she cursed silently. He disturbed her at a time when she had enough problems to deal with. She didn't need any more. And something told her Dr. Thorn Can-non could become a real problem.

Coming down the rest of the way, she handed him a set of keys. "The large key is for the front door. The rest are all labeled, so you shouldn't have any trouble figuring out what they're for."

He was being dismissed, but he wasn't ready to leave. He glanced at the empty living room again. "How long have you lived here?"

"Almost a year."

He jerked his head around to see if she was kidding. She wasn't. There was a challenge in her eyes, as though she were defying him to comment on her lack of furniture. She was right in that it wasn't any of his business how she lived. But he also saw something else in her eyes, an awareness he recognized because he felt it too.

The big question was what was he going to do about it?

There were other answers he wanted at the moment. "I remember some of the kids used to call this Old Man Baskin's Haunted House."

"Oliver Baskin was my grandfather. He left me this house and some other property in town."

"Did your grandfather have something against furniture?"

"Just the opposite. There was enough furniture here to furnish three homes. My grandfather saved everything from old soda pop bottles to issues of *National Geographic* dating back thirty years. Some of the cobwebs were older than I am. It was easier just to have everything removed."

Thorn looked back at the empty room. She had cleared away the past but hadn't provided any furnishings for the present. He wondered why.

Before he could ask any further questions, she said, "Edith will be phoning about eight o'clock our time tomorrow night."

He nodded. Placing his aunt's house keys in his

pocket, he said, "I'll be back tomorrow night, then."
He paused. "If that's all right with you."

"I have a feeling it's the only way you're going to
be satisfied your aunt is all right."

He wanted to touch her. Just to touch her, to
prove to himself she was real and not a figment of
his imagination. Raising his hand with the inten-
tion of stroking the soft flesh along her jawline, he
was startled to see her eyes widen in shock. She
took a step back from him as though his hand were
a flame and she didn't want to get burned.

He dropped his hand to his side. Something didn't
make sense. Why did she not like being touched,
even though standing practically naked in front of
him hadn't bothered her one bit? The two reactions
conflicted strangely. His own reaction to her wasn't
normal either. He needed time to think about everything he had experienced today.

Walking to the door, he said, "I'll see you tomorrow."

Rachel watched him leave, listening to his footsteps fade. She didn't move until she heard his car
start.

As she walked toward the kitchen, it occurred to
her she should have invited him to stay to dinner.
Ruby's Café closed at five o'clock, and there was no
other restaurant within fifteen miles. There wasn't
all that much food in her refrigerator, but more
than he would find at Edith's. His aunt had gotten
rid of all perishables before she left.

Thorn wasn't thinking about food as he drove away
though. His curiosity concerning Rachel Hyatt was
piqued. To say he was attracted to her was an un-
derstatement. He knew very little about her except
her name, but he knew he was intrigued by this

strange woman. She was a paradox, a beautiful woman who drove an expensive sports car, yet lived in sleepy, small-town Bowersville, Iowa, with no furniture in her house.

It didn't make any more sense than his aunt's suddenly getting married. Before the weekend was over he was going to have some answers. And not only about his aunt.

Two

Rachel was drinking her second cup of coffee the following morning when her agent, Henry Avery, phoned from New York. Originally his agency had handled her modeling bookings. When she switched careers to create the comic strip "Fancy Fannie," Henry represented her with the newspaper syndicates, and now dealt with all the merchandising offers for various products using Fannie's image. Henry was a good friend as well as an astute businessman. He was also stubborn. He couldn't understand why she couldn't manage to work in a few modeling assignments along with keeping up with her comic strip deadlines.

Ever since she had left New York, Henry had consistently and persistently contacted her with various offers for modeling jobs, finding it hard to believe she would voluntarily give up a lucrative career to live in Iowa of all places. As far as he was concerned, New York was the only civilized city in the United

States. He might not have approved of her decision to leave New York, but he had helped her make the move easier. He had even gone with her to buy a car before she left. And he had approved of her choice. The red Porsche was a gift she gave herself, a reward for all her years of hard work before getting her own comic strip.

This morning Henry had yet another offer for a modeling assignment, this one for a television commercial. As she had for the past year, Rachel turned down the assignment, then had to listen to Henry express his views on her sanity.

He was one of the few people who knew about her other career, the one she had given up modeling for to pursue full-time. Quitting modeling had been just about the easiest thing she had ever done. Being an extremely private person, Rachel had dreaded each fashion show and photography session.

As far as her grandfather was concerned, college was a waste of time and he wouldn't finance any further education for her once she graduated from high school. Whether he had expected her to come back to Bowersville to be his housekeeper or not had never been discussed. But then, few things were.

Her looks, she decided, were her only salable commodity. Since her grandfather considered his responsibility as a guardian was over once she turned eighteen, she had to use what she had. Her physical appearance was her best asset . . . and a liability when she tried to be taken seriously as a cartoonist.

The only way she could live with the idea of parading her body in front of cameras and strangers was to keep her privacy within herself. Such a condition might not make any sense to anyone else, but it did to her. It had been a defense mechanism as long as she could remember.

Modeling had been a way for her to make a living while she honed her craft as a cartoonist. Because of her youth, inexperience, and lack of formal training, no one had given her a second thought when she had tried time and again to have her work accepted. She continued modeling until "Fancy Fannie" was finally accepted by a newspaper syndicate under the name R. Dorsey. Now it was currently carried by newspapers all over the country.

She used her first initial and her middle name not because she was ashamed of what she was doing but because she wanted to preserve her anonymity. She didn't need public acclaim or recognition, nor did she want it. Her work was no one else's business except hers, the newspapers', and her agent's.

Once her strip was accepted, she had stayed in New York, mostly because she didn't have anywhere else to go. A few months later she had received word that her grandfather had died. After attending the funeral, she had learned she was his only heir. To her surprise and dismay, he had more extensive property than she had expected. In fact, he owned half the darn town of Bowersville.

It was absurd to think of trying to sell the land in Iowa from New York. She had packed up her clothes and drawing equipment and left New York without a single regret, moving back to Bowersville. In the beginning she had thought it would be only a temporary move. She would sell the land and then return to New York, or maybe move to a warmer climate. Things hadn't worked out that way.

She hadn't been able to unload even one of the

pieces of property as yet. There wasn't a great rush of people eager to settle in a small town where there was no industry. Until she could figure out what to do about her inheritance, she couldn't make any plans to move anywhere else.

Rachel carried her coffee mug into the sun room and sat down at her drawing board. The room had windows on three sides and one glass wall facing north, providing her with the best natural light for her artwork. After clearing the house of all the excess furniture and clutter, she had furnished only the rooms she used—a bedroom, the art studio, the kitchen, and one bathroom.

The area around her drafting table was utilitarian, with several high tables for her equipment and a stool for her to sit on. In the neighboring town she had bought many plants to decorate the sun room. Some were hanging and others were set on the floor along the glass wall to add color and life to the large rectangular room. A mobile of crystal dolphins hung from the ceiling, sending prisms of light around the room when it caught the sun.

She took her denim painting shirt off a hook behind the door and slipped it on over her white knit top. Her jeans were well-worn, soft, and comfortable, as were the moccasins she preferred to wear. She put on a pair of headphones and adjusted the volume of the small cassette player it was hooked into. Then she picked up a small sable brush and dipped it into a bottle of red ink. Before applying the ink to the storyboard in front of her to color in the bright vest Fannie was wearing, she pulled a pad over to make a few practice strokes to loosen up her hand. Usually she made swirls or quick sketches for a few minutes, like an athlete performing warmup exercises before competing in a race.

Suddenly she stopped. The sketch in front of her wasn't circles or stick figures. She stared. The lines on the pad depicted a strong masculine jawline, a chiseled nose, thick hair, and intelligent eyes. The drawing was a remarkable likeness to the man she had met yesterday. Thorn Cannon.

She tore the paper off the drawing board and crumpled it up. Some of the red ink was still wet and left marks on her hands. With a sound of disgust she tossed the ball of paper into the wastebasket. Pausing before she dipped the brush again into the ink, she wished dismissing Thorn Cannon from her mind would be as easy as wadding up his image and throwing it away.

The melodious voice of Carly Simon in her ears shut out the world, effectively isolating her. Forcing herself to concentrate on the sectioned-off squares and the figures she had drawn on the heavy paper tacked to the board, she began to apply the brush to the outline of Fannie's vest.

Lost in her work, she wasn't aware of how much time passed. The first indication she had of something not being quite right was an odd prickly sensation on the back of her neck. Lifting the brush off the paper, she slowly turned her head, looking over her shoulder toward the door.

Dressed in jeans and a red cotton sweater over a red and white striped shirt, Thorn was leaning against the door frame. She saw his lips move but couldn't hear what he said. She removed the earphones.

"What did you say?" she asked, shifting on the stool to face him.

His voice was warm yet guarded, as though he weren't sure of his reception. "Good morning, Rachel."

"Good morning, Dr. Cannon."

He frowned at the formal use of his name. "I can't very well ask you for a cup of coffee if you keep calling me Dr. Cannon. It makes me feel like I'm making a house call. I couldn't find anything resembling coffee in my aunt's cupboards. Just about a ton of tea bags."

Setting down the brush, she said casually, "This is the second time you've walked into this house without being invited."

"It's a nasty habit I'm trying to break. I did knock this time." His gaze shifted to the headphones she had placed on the drawing board. "Now I know why you didn't hear me."

"How long have you been standing there?"

He shrugged. "Does it matter?"

"I guess not." He'd already seen more than she wanted him to see. It was doubtful he would just ignore it.

Shoving himself away from the door, he walked over to the wall where she had hung a number of sketches. He studied each one, recognizing the main character in the drawings. "Fancy Fannie" was a diminutive Gypsy who traveled all over the world, getting involved in all sorts of adventures, some dangerous, some unusual, but all funny and unconventional. The character was extravagant in her dress and her actions, her humor dry and witty. Even Thorn's untrained eye could see the artistry in each stroke of the pen and the discipline required in creating clear, concise drawings.

There weren't many opportunities in his busy life for Thorn to read the daily paper, but he had read "Fancy Fannie" occasionally in the Sunday edition. He had enjoyed the sharp humor in the strip, the subtle cynicism in various episodes.

The part he was having trouble accepting was that Rachel Hyatt was R. Dorsey, the creator of the strip.

He walked over to the table where she still sat. "You're full of surprises, R. Dorsey. Why did you tell me your name was Rachel Hyatt?"

"Because it is my name. My full name is Rachel Dorsey Hyatt."

He picked up her hand, holding it with enough strength so she couldn't pull it away. His thumb stroked over her red-stained flesh. "I thought you'd cut yourself. I'm glad it's only ink. I'm also relieved you didn't just tell me Dorsey is your married name."

Rachel's expression was a mixture of confusion and irritation as she attempted to tug her hand out of his. His reaction wasn't what she had expected. He certainly didn't seem at all surprised to find out what she did. Even though she wasn't wild about him knowing about the strip, she felt a bit deflated that he didn't at least say he was impressed or even surprised.

He suddenly dropped her hand and picked up the mug she had left on a nearby table. "If I manage to find the kitchen, do you want me to bring you back some coffee?"

She pushed her stool away from the drawing table. "I'll get the coffee."

"I didn't mean to disturb your work. I'm perfectly capable of pouring a couple of cups of coffee. It's one of the first things they taught us at med school."

He disturbed her more than he could possibly guess, she thought. "I need a break anyway," she murmured as she walked out of the room.

The sound of his leather shoes was obscenely loud on the wooden floors as Thorn followed her down the hallway and through the empty dining room. A chandelier hung from the ceiling, its crystal prisms sparkling in the light that poured in through a large picture window.

Bringing his attention back to the woman ahead of him, he wondered for the tenth time what it was about Rachel Hyatt that drew him toward her. During the long night he had dismissed the attraction as a reaction to finding her naked in the river, a purely reflexive action of a healthy male. He'd been wrong.

He had walked into her house and found her bent over a drawing table. Even from the back the sight of her had caused his heart to race and his body to harden. Dressed in casual clothes, she could affect him as no other woman wearing a seductive gown had.

She pushed open the swinging door leading into the kitchen, and he caught it as it swung back toward him. Having seen the bare living room and dining room, and her sparsely furnished workroom, the kitchen was a revelation. He stood in the doorway and looked around. A bushy ivy plant hung over the window above the sink. The cupboards had been painted a light yellow, and there were yellow and blue plaid place mats set out on the round table in an alcove. Matching plaid material covered several small appliances sitting on the counter.

Rachel took down blue cups and saucers and set them on the counter. "Do you take anything in your coffee?"

"No." He came farther into the room. "Would I be pushing my luck if I asked for something to eat? Aunt Edith's cupboards make Mother Hubbard's look like a well-stocked supermarket. I gnawed on some stale crackers last night, which was all I could find to eat."

She turned around and looked at him for a moment. "It depends on how fussy you are. My cupboards are not exactly overflowing either."

He opened the refrigerator door and peered inside. "I see what you mean." He reached in and took out a container. "What's this?"

"Yogurt." She saw his face and laughed. "Not a yogurt fan, Dr. Cannon?"

He shook his head. "Not particularly. Was there a sale on orange juice? You have six containers of the stuff."

She set their cups on the table. "I like orange juice."

"Obviously." He made a sound of triumph. From behind the juice he withdrew a carton of eggs. As though the kitchen were his rather than hers, he set about fixing his breakfast. He began opening cupboards and drawers, finding what he needed, completely ignoring her.

Feeling superfluous, Rachel sat down at the table. Her chin cupped in her hand, she watched him crack a half dozen eggs in a bowl, then whip them with a fork, whistling under his breath. She didn't offer any help when he searched through the cupboards for a pan.

In a few minutes he had scrambled the eggs and portioned them out onto two plates, setting one in front of her. He poured two glasses of juice and brought them over to the table before sitting down across from her.

Lifting his glass, he made a toast. "To breakfast. The most important meal of the day."

She clinked her glass to his automatically. "I don't eat breakfast."

"You should eat breakfast. It's the most important meal of the day. I'm a doctor, remember? I know these things." He glanced at her hand with its vivid ink stains. "After you wash your hands."

She was tempted not to do as he suggested out of sheer perversity. Unfortunately he was right. She needed to wash her hands. She got up and washed them at the sink. While she dried them she said, "Edith mentioned you had a tendency to be bossy. She was right."

"It's odd how often being right gets confused with being bossy." He waited until she resumed her seat before he began to eat. "You know it isn't fair that you've heard about me from my aunt and she's never told me anything about you."

Rachel picked at her eggs. "You know more about me than Edith does."

Thorn stared at her, clearly surprised. "Edith doesn't know about R. Dorsey?"

She shook her head. "No one here does."

"Why not? If I could do something as creative as 'Fancy Fannie,' I wouldn't be hiding it."

Feeling defensive, Rachel said, "I'm not ashamed

of what I do. It's just that I don't think it's anyone else's business."

He didn't comment, his silence saying more than any words could.

She slammed her fork down onto the table. She rose from her chair, walked over to the sink, and whirled around. "I'm not ashamed of what I do."

He shifted in his chair, resting his arm over the back as he took in her defiant stance—chin raised, hands on her hips. She really was magnificent when she was angry. Golden lights of temper flashed in her eyes, and desire clenched in his gut as he reacted to the fire within her. He couldn't help wondering how she would feel under him, responding to the heat and need within him. She was a passionate woman who for some reason tried to hide the fact.

"I didn't say you were ashamed," he replied mildly. "Sit down and finish your breakfast. It's not a good idea to argue on an empty stomach."

"I'm not arguing. I'm trying to make a point."

"And you've made it. Your work is none of my business either. Now sit down and finish your breakfast before the eggs get cold."

His calm manner put an end to her anger as effectively as throwing ice water on hot coals. Feeling foolish, she returned to the table and sat down. He wasn't demanding any explanations, which was what she wanted. Or what she thought she wanted. There was something in the way he watched her as he sipped his coffee that disturbed her, confused her . . . and made her question what it was she really did want.

Her mind was so preoccupied by thoughts of Thorn,

she didn't even notice she was eating the scrambled eggs.

Thorn did, but he knew her well enough by now to know she wouldn't appreciate him rubbing it in. Casually he asked, "What else doesn't Edith know about you?"

"That's about it." It didn't occur to her to tell him or anyone else about her modeling career. It was the past, her past.

He shook his head, disagreeing with her. "I think there's a great deal more. You stick out in this little town like a rose among radishes."

Her shoulders lifted and fell in a dismissive gesture. "I'm no different from anyone else."

"And tofu is my favorite food," he said mockingly, clearly not believing her.

When he finished he took his plate over to the sink. Bringing the coffeepot back with him, he refilled their cups. "I appreciate the breakfast. If you had turned me away, I would have had to go to Ruby's Café and hear about Mrs. Lindstrom's bunions again. That is, if the café is even open."

"It opens at seven. Most of the people around here are early risers."

"I noticed. I went for a run at six and kept seeing curtains move in the windows of every house I passed. Cyrus Fitzroy, who used to chase me away from his apple trees, was sweeping off his porch and scowled at me. He probably thought I was going to go after his apples again."

Rachel smiled. She couldn't help it. His self-deprecating humor was too appealing to resist. "Jogging hasn't quite made it to Bowersville."

"There are a number of things that haven't quite

made it to Bowersville," he said dryly. "Nothing ever changes here. If a car backfires, it's a major event."

"I think that's what most of the residents like."

He leaned back in his chair. "Is that why you live here?"

She picked up her plate and took it over to the sink. "There are worse places to be."

The front two legs of his chair left the floor as he leaned back even farther. As he watched her, he could almost see her adding another brick to the wall she erected around herself. He knew it was there but not why. Nor did he know why she buried herself away in this small community. Or hid her identity as the creator of a popular comic strip. Or lived in a practically empty house.

Or why just looking at her heated his blood.

It was pure pleasure to watch her do the simplest thing, like rinsing her plate. Each movement of her hands and the way she held herself had a certain charm. Her tall, sleek body could make even the most informal clothes appear classy—and sexy as hell.

There was another attraction. Under the self-sufficient, cool woman was a vulnerable, passionate one. It was the woman underneath who intrigued him and kept drawing him toward her.

He returned the chair to its proper position. A sudden restlessness edged along his nerve endings. He needed to take his mind off how she would feel under his hands and concentrate on other things or he was going to do something incredibly stupid.

He stood up and finished clearing the table. "I've never had breakfast with a justice of the peace before."

"That makes us even. I've never had anyone cook my breakfast before."

If he was startled by her last statement, his expression gave no indication. Leaning a hip against the counter, he said, "You're still one up on me. You've met a doctor before. I've never known a cartoonist or a justice of the peace. I'll tell you why I've become a doctor if you'll tell me why you're the justice of the peace."

Rachel dried her hands on a towel and looked at him. The humor reflected in his eyes and the slight curve of his mouth acted like a magnet, drawing her deeper into the attraction she was finding difficult to fight. There hadn't been all that many people with a sense of humor in her life for her to take them for granted.

"It's not that big a deal," she said. "I didn't want to have to keep driving to Algona every time I needed a notary. When I applied to become one myself, the clerk gave me an application for a justice of the peace. I didn't notice until I received my appointment from the state. As it turned out, there hasn't been a need to have anything notarized since I haven't been able to find any buyers for the property my grandfather left me."

"Why did my aunt have you officiate at her wedding? Why didn't she opt for a church wedding?"

"There was a difference in religion between Edith and Taylor, so they compromised and had a civil ceremony." She paused. "The marriage is legal. When she asked me to marry them, I checked all the rules and regulations to make sure I would do everything correctly."

Thorn frowned, crossing his arms over his chest

and looking off into space. "I still don't understand why she couldn't have let me know she was getting married. It's not like her."

Rachel took the opportunity to study him while his attention was elsewhere. Even though she had met him only yesterday, she knew a great deal about him from his devoted aunt. Edith had given her the details, such as his years of studying for his medical degree and his earlier education courtesy of a military school. She knew some of the facts pertaining to his life but not how he felt about any of them.

It dawned on her as she watched him that he was actually hurt by his aunt neglecting to notify him of her wedding. He didn't give anything away in his expression, yet somehow she sensed how he was feeling. Her perception surprised her. All of her reactions to Thorn disturbed her. It was crazy to feel so strongly about a man she had just met.

It would be even crazier to become involved with him.

"When you talk to Edith tonight," she said, "you can find out everything you want to know."

Thorn glanced at his watch. It was only nine o'clock. "Do you have any suggestions as to what I can do until tonight?"

She smiled faintly. "You can borrow my fishing pole."

He was silent for a moment as he considered her suggestion. He would rather spend the day with her, but she obviously didn't have the desire to be with him.

He shrugged. "Why not? I haven't been fishing for years. It's better than wandering around my aunt's house or keeping you from your work." Or fighting the desire to pull her into his arms.

Rachel stepped around him and walked to the back door. "I'll get my fishing gear for you."

Thorn accompanied her to the garage. Except for her car and the fishing equipment, the building was stripped of gardening tools and the assorted clutter usually found in garages. She had cleared out this part of the property too.

Accepting the bamboo fishing pole from her, he examined it with a puzzled frown. "You wouldn't have anything resembling a fishing rod from this century, would you?"

She smiled. "Sorry."

"If I figure out how to work this thing and catch some fish, I'll share them with you if you cook them."

"Are you inviting yourself to dinner?"

"Sounds that way."

She shook her head in exasperation. "Did anyone ever tell you you're a very pushy person?"

"Maybe once or twice."

"Make it three times."

His smile deepened. "So, will you cook the fish?"

"What if you don't catch any?"

He gave her a pained look. "You don't have much faith in my ability as a fisherman."

"You said yourself you haven't been fishing for a long time."

He helped her slide the garage door shut, grunting as the door scraped roughly in its track. Brushing off his hands, he picked up the gear again. "If I don't catch anything for our dinner, I'll stop at Peabody's and pick up a couple of steaks."

As she walked beside him to his car, she sighed

with resignation. "I've lived in Iowa long enough to know there isn't anything that can be done about a tornado except to ride it out."

He opened the car door. Folding his arms on the top of it, he asked, "Is that what you're going to do? Ride out this weekend?"

"It's either that or hide under a table until it blows over and you leave."

In a gesture that surprised them both, Thorn reached out and stroked the soft skin of her throat with the back of his knuckles. "It's liable to be a rough ride. The way you make me feel isn't calm."

His touch sent spirals of heat searing through her. "Thorn, I—"

He caught the startled expression in her eyes and again marveled at her stunned response when he touched her. At least this time she hadn't moved away from him. Cupping her face, he brushed her lips with his thumb, effectively halting her words. His voice was softly serious. "Tell me you don't feel the same attraction and I'll back off."

It should have been easy to tell him she wasn't interested. A simple no was all she would have to say. He didn't have to know how her pulse rate accelerated when she saw him, or the way her skin became sensitized when he was near her.

As her eyes met his, she wondered why she couldn't lie to him.

When she didn't answer, he moved his hand to the back of her neck, slowly drawing her toward him. The car door was between them, but he didn't change his position, purposely allowing the barrier. His gaze never left her face as he brought her against the door and lowered his head.

Changing his earlier demand, he said, "*Show* me you don't feel the same attraction and I'll back off."

His mouth covered hers with an immediate hunger. Rachel froze. A helpless longing ripped through her as his kiss demanded a response from her. Unable to resist, she gave in without thought of the consequences. The world splintered around her, then centered on just the two of them. Her hands came up to grip the edge of the car door as though she needed something solid to hold, to anchor her in reality.

Thorn broke open her mouth and slid his tongue into her velvet warmth. The heat and taste of her sent jagged shafts of need deep within him, hardening his loins and his intent. He reluctantly raised his head, breaking the contact between them. Then he tormented himself further by briefly touching her lips with his again in a gentle caress more devastating than his first hungry assault.

He relaxed his hold on her, although he didn't completely release her. Looking down at her, he saw the dazed passion in the depths of her dark eyes.

Tenderness. He hadn't expected to feel it for her. Or expected to want it for himself. Passion and need were familiar reactions he could recognize and understand. The desire to cherish and protect welled up inside him, changing the way he held her delicate neck. His thumb stroked the soft skin, his gaze sliding from her slightly swollen lips to the pulse beating madly at the base of her throat.

He had his answer. Rachel was the missing link in his life, one he hadn't known wasn't there. Just being with her completed him somehow, made him feel whole.

Rachel blinked and took a deep shuddering breath. She loosened her grip on the door and slowly withdrew from his possessive hold. The need to protect herself was strong, as though she had been too close to a raging fire and had almost been burned. She couldn't get rid of the feeling she had given part of herself to Thorn and he had accepted it. Now she was afraid she wouldn't be the same without him.

Shaking her head slowly, she denied what had happened between them. "No," she whispered, backing away from him.

He smiled gently. Her reaction wasn't totally unexpected. "Afraid so. You have all day to get used to it."

She watched him fold his long length into the car. She couldn't imagine ever getting used to the painful pleasure she had found in his touch. How could he calmly go fishing when everything had changed so drastically in such a short period of time, she wondered as he backed out of the drive.

If he thought she could figure out what she was going to do in only one day, he expected a lot of a few hours.

Three

When Thorn returned to Rachel's later in the afternoon, he put the fishing equipment back into the garage before walking toward the house. Instead of a string of fish, he carried two steaks wrapped in white butcher paper.

Crossing the lawn between the garage and the house, he heard a rhythmic creaking sound. Curious, he walked around to the side of the house. Hanging from a large tree branch was an old wooden porch swing. Sitting on the swing was Rachel. Her foot casually kicked the ground to keep the swing in motion.

Her attention was on a couple of maple leaves she was holding in her lap, so he was able to observe her without her being aware of his presence. She had changed her clothes and was now wearing a creamy yellow cotton knit dress loosely gathered at the waist with a braided leather belt. A slight breeze ruffled the brown curls resting on her shoulders and the full skirt hanging over the seat.

As he gazed at her, Thorn could feel himself being drawn to her like metal filings to a magnet. While he had been gone, her image had stayed in his mind and had affected his body. Ever since he had seen her in the river, he had been in a state of low arousal that didn't ease when he was away from her.

The way she had overcome her reluctance to be touched and had responded to his kiss had left him aching all afternoon. In only two days she had replaced all other women he'd ever known.

Rachel didn't stop the motion of the swing when she looked up and saw Thorn. She hoped she appeared cool and faintly friendly, although inside, her stomach clenched and her heartbeat accelerated uncomfortably. For a moment she simply stared at him, then she smiled when she saw the white package in his hand.

"Well, darn," she said in mock dismay. "I had my heart set on fresh fish for dinner."

"It was either the antique bamboo pole, the bait, or me they didn't like. Not one single fish wanted to come home with me."

"I wouldn't take it personally. There are some stubborn fish in the river."

He stopped several feet away from the swing, his eyes never leaving her. Feeling self-conscious under his intense gaze, she asked, "Why are you looking at me like that? It's not my fault you didn't catch any fish."

His voice was soft. "You look as though you belong on the cover of *Vogue*. I can't figure out why you've settled here where the average age of the residents is sixty. It doesn't make any sense."

"It doesn't have to make sense to you, only to me."

A long, tense silence stretched between them. Thorn felt impatient and frustrated as she made it clear she wasn't removing any of the bricks in the wall around her. Using the discipline ingrained in him during his long years of medical school and internship, he tamped down his anger and reached for patience.

The swing ceased its movement as he sat down beside her. "Are you through working for the day?"

"Yes." She sighed deeply. "It might sound odd, but after working long hours on the strip, I'm exhausted even though I've done nothing more strenuous than lift a pen. When I'm finished for the day, I take a long soak in the tub, then come out here." She started the swing to swaying again. "What do you do after a day of poking and prodding people in the name of medicine?"

His smile was slightly crooked. "You have an odd concept of a doctor's duties. It depends on what kind of day I had. If there have been emergencies long into the night, I fall into bed the minute I get to my apartment. If it's been a light day, I occasionally go to the gym to work out or go out to dinner somewhere quiet."

Rachel twirled a leaf around by its stem as she wondered whether he usually had female company when he went out to dinner. It hadn't mattered before with any other man. It shouldn't matter now with him.

He picked up the leaf that still lay on her lap. "You

might as well know now. I hate those restaurants where they have a loud band. Discos are not at the top of my list either."

She considered his statement. Since Bowersville didn't have either a loud band or a disco, his preferences weren't going to matter during his short stay in town.

"I promise no loud music while we're having dinner."

Thorn looked around. Trees and shrubs were abundant around the property, effectively shielding the yard and house from the neighbors. The only sound to intrude on the peace was the creaking of the chains holding the swing and the gentle rustle of leaves as an occasional breeze blew through them. No children's laughter, traffic noise, or any other indication of life going on around them could be heard.

"When I'm away from Bowersville," he said softly, "I forget how quiet the town is. It's like stepping into a vacuum. I was here only for several weeks each year. I can't imagine what you found to do for a whole summer when you were young."

Surprising both of them, Rachel gave away a piece of her past. "Do you see that big oak tree over there in the corner of the yard?"

He looked where she pointed. "What about it?"

"I used to have a platform in that fork of the tree where those three thick branches meet. In the summer the leaves would hide it from view. I wanted to build a small house up there, but all I could manage was to pound some boards together to make a floor. I spent many hours up there, reading and sketching."

"Why didn't you ask your grandfather to build you walls and a roof?"

"I never told him about it. At the time I thought it was my secret place, but he must have known it was there. I didn't think he would understand why I needed a place of my own when I had a perfectly good room in his house. Later, when I knew him better, I realized he would have understood."

Thorn was silent for a few minutes. Her childhood sounded lonely in the extreme. It was difficult to imagine Rachel living with Old Man Baskin, who could scare leaves off trees just by walking under the branches.

Whether to comfort her or himself, he took her hand, resting their clasped fingers on her lap. He craved the physical contact with her, even if it was only holding her hand, to ease the desire coiling tightly through him.

"Is that why I don't remember seeing you when I was here visiting my aunt? Except for the time you said I put a frog down your sweater. You spent most of your summers up in a tree?"

Rachel's heart had thudded painfully in her chest when he laced his fingers through hers in a gesture that was anything but casual to her. In the short time she'd known him, she had discovered he was a tactile person. Holding, stroking, touching were all normal ways for him to communicate. As a physician, it was a necessary diagnostic tool. As a man, it was devastatingly potent.

Dragging her mind back from the intimacy of his hand resting on her thigh, she said quietly, "Being alone when I was a child wasn't as odd as you make it sound. Like my grandfather, I tended to prefer my own company. I still do. You might remember my grandfather as Old Man Baskin who lived in a haunted house, but he was kind to me in his own way. It's true he wasn't one of Bowersville's more sociable citizens, but he wanted it like that. It couldn't have been easy for him to be stuck with a young girl after my parents were killed in a car accident."

"It couldn't have been all that easy for you either. I remember seeing him only once. I accidentally bumped into him when I was coming out of Peabody's and he was going in. He didn't speak to me—he growled."

A corner of her mouth lifted. "You probably deserved it."

"I'll have you know I was extremely polite," he replied, mildly affronted. "I apologized for running into him, and he nearly took my head off."

It was easy to imagine Thorn's reaction. It had been similar to her own when she had first met her grandfather. "Your aunt was one of the few people who wasn't intimidated by his rough manner. She would bring him a freshly baked cake or a casserole and dare him to eat it. He would grudgingly accept whatever she brought. Sometimes he would sit out here with her on this swing, neither one of them saying a word for the longest time. Then she would go home." She smiled. "She always brought me a huge round cookie, as big as a saucer."

"Chocolate chip with a happy face painted on it in yellow frosting. Edith called them Happy Cookies."

She nodded. "I kept the first one until it became hard as a rock. It was so big and so pretty, and I didn't know she would bring me another one. The next one I made last for over a week. She still makes them, and I still enjoy them."

Thorn had grown up taking the Happy Cookies for granted, and Rachel had kept one as though it were a prized possession. "She brought me one six months ago when she came to Des Moines for a visit. It was the hit of my medical staff and quite a few of the patients."

"Taylor enjoyed them too. She made a batch before they left for Hawaii."

"Ah, yes. I almost forgot about good old Taylor, my aunt's new husband."

Rachel didn't want to have a repeat of their quarrel concerning his aunt's marriage. She had enjoyed the last few minutes and didn't want them spoiled. With her foot she stopped the swing's motion and tugged her hand out of his.

"If you want something to eat before Edith phones, I'd better get started fixing dinner." She held out her hand for the package of steaks.

Instead of handing her the meat, Thorn stood and drew her up with him. "I'll help."

His idea of helping was to basically take over. It was obvious he knew his way around a kitchen and could prepare meals other than breakfast. Rachel set the table and watched him.

He had just put the steaks under the broiler when the phone rang. It was too early for the call from his aunt, but since he was closest to the phone, he answered it. For a few seconds the person at the other end of the phone didn't say anything. Finally a man's voice asked to speak to Rachel Hyatt.

Thorn handed the phone to her and went back to the counter to prepare a spinach salad. He unabashedly listened to Rachel's end of the conversation, although he couldn't make much sense of it. Rachel asked if there was any damage, then agreed to see someone after school on Monday.

When she hung up, she took a notebook out of a drawer and jotted something down in it.

Turning the steaks, Thorn asked, "What was that all about?"

She closed the book and put it away. "It's nothing. Those steaks smell wonderful. How much longer will it be before they're ready?"

"Another minute or so. Who are you going to see on Monday?"

Using the theory that the best defense is a strong offense, Rachel countered with a question of her own. "What difference could it possibly make to you? You'll be back in Des Moines by then."

Thorn crossed his arms and continued to look at her. "Along with being incredibly bossy, I'm also extremely stubborn. It will be easier if you just tell me what I want to know."

Making a dismissing gesture with her hand, she muttered, "It's really no big deal."

"Then there's no reason why you can't tell me about it, is there?"

"I suppose not," she said with resignation. "I'll tell you about the phone call if you'll take the steaks out of the broiler before they become charcoal briquets."

Thorn removed the steaks and set them on the plates at the table. Taking her arm, he escorted her to the table and pulled out her chair for her. With an exaggerated flick of her napkin, he spread it on her lap, then walked around the table and sat down.

"Madam has her steak now."

A corner of her mouth twitched. "I can see that."

Keeping her part of the bargain, she explained, "As you know, there is no police department in Bowersville. The mayor usually settles minor infractions or disagreements, but he's recuperating from a heart attack. I'm the only justice of the peace in town, so I get called on once in a while to deal with the occasional law violation."

"You're going to see a kid who broke the law?"

"During the summer Tony Thompson worked on a farm and used the money he made to buy himself an old truck. He's souped it up, and likes to see how fast he can go on the country roads. His father has received several complaints from residents about his speeding before, but yesterday he knocked down a farmer's mailbox. Apparently his father has decided someone else might have more success in reprimanding the boy. I'm it."

Would she ever stop surprising him, he wondered. From the first moment he had seen her he had been intrigued and mystified by her more than he was comfortable with. "What are you going to say to the kid when you see him?"

"It depends on his attitude." She glanced at his plate. "You aren't eating."

His hunger for more knowledge about her was stronger than any desire for food. Nevertheless, he began to eat. "You said earlier you spent your summers here with your grandfather. Where did you live the rest of the year?"

"I attended a boarding school in the east."

The flat statement had his eyes narrowing as he studied her face. No wonder she was so self-contained, he thought. She had been essentially on her own since she was a child. He couldn't imagine how she must have felt being shipped off to an unfamiliar school to live with strangers. Then she spent her summers with a man who lived like a hermit.

"What about holidays, your birthday?" he asked. "Didn't you spend Christmas with your grandfather?"

"No."

Another short answer. He knew he was pushing, but he couldn't help it. "So how did Santa Claus find you?"

She smiled faintly. "Santa Claus sent me a check. Actually it was a money order. My grandfather didn't trust banks enough to put his money in them."

"Did you stay at the boarding school during the holidays?"

"Sometimes. Occasionally I went home with a friend to spend the holidays with her and her family. It was like stepping into another world. A very noisy world. One friend had six brothers and sisters. I had to watch where I walked and learn to lock the bathroom door."

"And had the time of your life?"

Her smile widened. "It was definitely different."

Thorn studied her. He was beginning to understand her reaction when he touched her. She had been startled, even faintly alarmed, although she had tried to hide it. There couldn't have been much affection handed out by Old Man Baskin when she was young and vulnerable. Apparently, as an adult, she hadn't let anyone close enough to the sensitive woman he was discovering under her cool exterior.

He was about to ask her what she had done after leaving school and before coming back to Bowersville, but he wasn't given a chance. The sound of someone knocking at the front door had Rachel pushing herself away from the table.

The swinging door swished softly after she left the kitchen. A minute later she pushed it open again and he saw she wasn't alone. With her was a man whose age could have been anywhere from sixty to a hundred. Slightly stooped, he wore blue denim overalls, a tweed coat, and a gray and white striped railroad cap. He was easily carrying a bushel basket full of ears of corn.

"Thorn, do you remember Mr. Grundy, your aunt's neighbor?"

Setting the basket down, the elderly man offered Thorn a gnarled hand to shake as Thorn pushed back his chair and stood up. "It's good to see you, Mr. Grundy."

"Haven't seen you around much, young man. Also haven't had any broken windows lately either. Don't suppose the two things are related, do you?"

Thorn grinned. "Mr. Grundy, I didn't think you were the type of man to hold a grudge. I broke only one of your windows, and I remember mowing your lawn and weeding your garden to pay for it." Wanting to change the subject from his childhood indiscretions, he said, "I talked to you on the phone yesterday when I called about my aunt."

Mr. Grundy nodded abruptly. "So you did. I told you she weren't here. Gone off to one of them tropical islands."

Slanting a glance in Rachel's direction, Thorn saw the glint of amusement in her eyes. Mr. Grundy was making it clear he thought it was stupid of Thorn to have come to Bowersville when he had been told his aunt wasn't there.

"I brought you some popcorn," Mr. Grundy said, gesturing toward the basket of corn. "Every summer when you came to stay, your aunt always made sure she had plenty of popcorn on hand. Said you liked it. I was going to bring it over to your aunt's house this morning, but you left before I could get over there. Myrtle Simpson said you was over here."

Thorn had forgotten how difficult it was to do anything in the small town without everyone knowing about it. Too often when he was younger, his aunt would know he was doing something he shouldn't almost at the time he was doing it.

His gaze slid to the basket. There was enough corn to last him a year. "Thanks, Mr. Grundy," he said, bringing his gaze back to Mr. Grundy's lined face. "I appreciate the popcorn."

"Think nothing of it." He briefly grasped the bill of his cap as he mumbled, "Good day, Rachel."

She walked with him to the door, leaving Thorn with his popcorn. When she returned, he was examining one of the ears.

"Mr. Grundy takes great pride in his popcorn," she said. "Says it's the best in the state."

"It was nice of him to bring it over. I'm just not sure what I'm going to do with all of it." He placed the ear of corn back in the basket. Facing her, he asked quietly, "Is my being here with you going to cause you any problems? The whole town apparently knows we're together."

He could cost her a great deal, she thought, but not the way he meant. She shook her head. "The townspeople aren't malicious or snoopy." A breath of a laugh escaped her. "At first I thought that's exactly what they were. But now I know they simply care."

"But will your reputation be blackened by being paired off with me?"

"I'm not being paired off with anybody." She walked over to the table and picked up her plate. Taking it to the sink, she said, "We're sharing a meal, that's all."

He stopped her from returning to the table by taking her wrist. "Is it?"

She faced him squarely. With more force than necessary, she said, "Yes, that's all."

He didn't believe her. He felt an undeniable need to prove her wrong. Drawing her up against him, he lowered his head. She tried to pull away, but he wouldn't let her. His fingers combed through her hair to hold her head still. His lips caressed and cajoled, persuading her to accept him. Pleasure washed over him, and he deepened the kiss.

When the force of his mouth parted her lips, Rachel's resistance disintegrated. She leaned into him, her fingers clenching his shirt as his tongue invaded and explored her mouth. Desire welled up like a flood, overpowering her. Passion had been only a word in the past. Now it was real and more necessary than breathing.

He dragged her lower body to his, arousing them both with the intimate contact. The hard planes of his body were pressed tightly into her softer curves. She hadn't expected such a fierce longing to touch and be touched rising up like a flood after a dam had broken wide open.

Her scent surrounded him, engulfing him as he

devoured her mouth and immersed himself in her taste. He felt his control slip dangerously when her teeth scraped across his bottom lip and her hips ground against his. He knew he had to stop but wasn't sure he could.

He broke away from her mouth and buried his lips against her throat. Her pulse was beating as madly as his own.

"We fit together," he murmured. "I wondered if we would yesterday by the river. Now I know."

Shaken by the intensity of the last few moments, they drew apart. Thorn's gaze locked with hers. Feeling the need for support, Rachel stepped back and leaned against the counter.

With as much dignity as possible under the circumstances, she muttered, "So what was your point?"

Thorn didn't think it was possible to shift from passion to amusement so quickly, but he found himself choking back a laugh. "Never mind. I think I made it."

"Well, it really doesn't matter. You'll be returning to your patients tomorrow and my patience is about used up."

His pulse rate was still racing, yet he found himself smiling at her. "Do we go to neutral corners until my aunt calls?"

He was leaving it up to her, she thought. "You make it sound as though we're involved in some sort of contest."

Suddenly serious, he said quietly, "I don't know what it is, but we're definitely involved."

Rachel attempted to deny it. "I don't know about you, but I'm not interested in having a brief affair.

You have your life in Des Moines, and I have mine here. Let's leave it at that."

He didn't want to admit she was right, not the way he was feeling. He had always prided himself on being a practical man. The smart thing would be to stick to his original plans. He would talk to his aunt and make sure she was all right. Then he would return to Des Moines . . . and try to forget Rachel Hyatt.

Accepting his silence as agreement, Rachel turned back to the table to finish clearing off their plates. Neither had eaten much. She took the plates over to the trash and scraped the leftover steaks and salad into the bin.

Thorn watched her for a few minutes. Her usually graceful movements were oddly jerky as she moved around the kitchen. She dropped one of the forks and bent down to pick it up, only to drop it again. It didn't require a medical degree to realize she was more upset by what had happened than she was going to admit.

"Rachel," he said quietly, "do you want me to go?"

Retrieving the fork from the floor, she straightened and looked at him, a puzzled expression on her face. "I thought you wanted to talk to your aunt."

"I do, but I'm obviously making you uncomfortable."

Her step was slow and hesitant as she walked over to the sink. Placing the fork into the sink, she turned to face him. "It isn't you. I'm uncomfortable with the way you make me feel."

Her blunt honesty stunned him. She deserved the same from him. "If it makes you feel any better, I'm a little off balance myself."

"Well, it doesn't really matter one way or the other, does it? We can put it down to chemistry or physical attraction, or maybe a full moon. Maybe we should treat it like a rash. If you don't scratch it, eventually it will go away."

Thorn didn't care for her comparison, but he wasn't going to argue with her. "I need something to do to keep my hands busy so I don't start scratching the itch. Do you have some sort of container I can use? I can't imagine anything less arousing than shucking popcorn."

For the next hour Thorn sat at the table rubbing one ear of corn against another over a tin container. After Rachel finished cleaning the kitchen, she pulled a chair around and helped him. There were still a dozen ears of corn in the basket at eight o'clock. When the phone didn't ring, they kept on until the basket was completely empty and the tin was almost full.

Rachel made a pot of coffee while they waited, pacing the floor after a while as the phone still remained silent. By nine o'clock she was beginning to worry. Several times she picked up the phone to make sure it was still working. It was.

Thorn came back from depositing his tin of popcorn into the trunk of his car and saw her hang up the phone. "A watched pot never boils."

"This isn't a pot. It's a stupid phone that isn't ringing when it's supposed to," she said irritably. "I wonder if Edith got mixed up about the time change between here and Hawaii."

"Did she happen to leave the name of the hotel where she would be staying, or did they just hop on a plane to take whatever they could get when they arrived? We could call her."

Feeling foolish because she hadn't thought of it, Rachel opened the kitchen drawer and took out her notebook. Leafing through it, she found the page she wanted. "Here it is. The Outrigger East. I don't have the number, but I'll call the operator."

It didn't take long to get the number. It took a great deal longer for Rachel to get the information about Edith's room, however. The hotel had no record of Mr. and Mrs. Taylor Mead staying there. After questioning the clerk further, Rachel discovered the newlyweds had checked out the previous day.

When she told Thorn what she had learned, he took over the phone. He kept the operator busy getting the numbers for the Honolulu police, all the hospitals on the island of Oahu, and the airport. An hour later he slammed down the phone, exasperation in every line of his body.

"She can't have just disappeared off the face of the earth. Where in the hell can she be?"

"I don't know." When she saw him bang his fist on the counter, she grabbed his arm, unaware of the natural way she had reached out to comfort him. "She's perfectly capable of taking care of herself, Thorn. You know that."

"What about her new husband? He should be taking care of her."

She could feel the tension in his arm. "The explanation could be as simple as they decided to tour some of the other islands."

"What about her promise to phone you tonight?"

"Maybe she forgot or got confused about the time.

She'll call. Maybe not tonight but eventually." She hoped she sounded more confident than she felt.

He pulled away from her, picked up the phone, and called directory information again.

"Who are you calling now?"

She got her answer when he asked the operator for the numbers for several airlines. When he began to stab at the buttons again, she walked over to him.

"What are you doing?" she asked.

"I'm going to make a reservation to fly to Hawaii."

Reaching across him, she disconnected the call. Hard fingers closed around her wrist and he pulled her hand away from the phone. "What in hell are you doing?" he said.

His grip hurt, but she held her ground. "I'm stopping you from doing something stupid."

He flung her arm away from him and strode across the room. Whirling around, he said savagely,, "What would you know about what is stupid? You offici- ated at a wedding between a seventy-two-year-old woman and a man she's known for only a couple of weeks. Don't talk to me about stupid actions."

He was taking his anger and frustration out on her, and she didn't deserve it. "I didn't force your aunt to get married. If you think anyone can make Edith do anything she doesn't want to do, you don't know her at all. You should be happy for her. She's found someone to spend the rest of her life with. Being alone at any age is not all that wonderful. At seventy-two it has to be frightening."

"She would be safe if she had stayed here. He could have run out on her, leaving her stranded in Hawaii."

Leaning her hip against the counter, she asked, "What are you really afraid of, Thorn? That Edith is ill, or that Taylor Mead is going to spend all those millions?"

Fury welled up inside him, blinding him for a moment. His hands clenched tightly, his fingernails digging into his palms as his eyes drilled into her.

Before he said or did anything he might regret, he turned and walked to the back door, shutting it softly behind him.

Rachel slumped against the counter. She might just have accomplished more than she had set out to do.

Four

There were a lot of places she would rather be than knocking on Edith Warwick Mead's door at seven on a Sunday morning in the pouring rain. It hadn't been raining when she left her house, so she didn't have an umbrella, only the light slicker she had thrown on. She was wet from head to toe and getting wetter. This was not exactly a terrific way to start the day.

After what she had said to him the previous night, Thorn wasn't going to be real thrilled to see her either.

She lifted the door knocker again and struck the door several more times. Considering the hour, it wouldn't be unheard of for him to be in bed. Or he could be out jogging. His car was parked in the driveway, so she knew he hadn't returned to Des Moines. If he was still in bed, he could darn well get up. Her sleep had been interrupted by his aunt at three in the morning. It seemed only fair his slumber should be disturbed too. If he was jogging, she'd wait.

After about the tenth knock she heard the lock being unbolted. The hinges protested slightly as the door opened slowly.

Thorn had stopped to put on a pair of jeans before coming to the door, but not a shirt. He was lean yet muscular, his chest covered lightly with dark, curling hair. He needed a shave, his hair was tousled, and he didn't look at all cheerful or welcoming. Just incredibly sexy.

For a minute he simply looked at her. At last, in a voice husky with sleep, he asked, "Did you think of something else you neglected to throw at me last night?"

"No. I have some news about your aunt." When he didn't change expression or position, she said, "It might have escaped your notice, Dr. Cannon, but it happens to be raining this morning."

His gaze shifted to the steadily falling rain. "So it is. I'm sure the farmers will appreciate it."

"I'm soaking wet."

He looked at her. "You certainly are."

She had met some stubborn people in her life, but Thorn was definitely in the top ten of all-time obstinate men. If he was expecting an apology for what she had said the previous night, he would have a long wait.

She tried another tactic and held up the thermos she was carrying. "I brought coffee."

His gaze lingered on the thermos. Apparently some things were more important than pride, for he stepped aside to let her enter the house. She brushed by him and headed for the large country kitchen.

Once there, she removed her jacket and slung it over the back of a chair before reaching for a towel to dry her hands and face. She dabbed at her hair, then gave it up as a lost cause.

Thorn hadn't followed her, but she poured coffee into two cups anyway and set them on the table in the small nook in front of a window. On the sill were several small violet plants set in ceramic containers, their blossoms in a variety of soft shades. After testing the dry soil with her finger, she got a watering can and filled it at the sink.

She was watering the violets when Thorn entered the kitchen. He had put on a shirt and was buttoning it. Tucking the shirttails into his jeans, he asked, "To what do I owe this early morning assault?"

"If you don't want the coffee, just say so."

He was still stinging from her crack about his being more concerned about his aunt's money than his aunt herself, but he badly needed a cup of coffee. If it was a peace offering, he was more than willing to accept it.

Except she didn't seem to be in a particularly peaceful mood.

Rachel replaced the watering can under the sink, then turned to look at him. "Edith is all right."

"How do you know that?"

"She finally phoned at three this morning. She apologized for not calling last night. They had just been too busy."

"Doing what?"

She strolled over to the table and sat down. "That's exactly what I asked her." She took a sip of coffee and watched as he sat down across from her.

He leaned his arms on the table, obviously irritated. "Well? What did she say?"

"I was waiting for you to sit down before I told you."

"I'm sitting," he said, striving for patience. "Tell me."

"Edith and Taylor went on a tour of the other islands and fell in love with the island of Maui. To condense what was a very long story, they've bought a house on Maui and plan to stay there."

Thorn's expression was one of disbelief and shock.

Rachel smiled grimly. "There's more."

"I'm not sure I want to hear it."

"Sorry. This isn't multiple choice. You have to hear all of it. They don't plan on coming back to Bowersville. She gave me a list of things she wants me to send to her. Mostly clothes and a couple of pieces of furniture. Some personal items and, of course, all the pictures of her beloved nephew. She asked me to get in touch with you to tell you this house was now yours. When I told her you were here, she sounded extremely pleased with herself, saying something about things working out better than she had hoped, whatever that means."

She slid her hand into the back pocket of her jeans and withdrew a slip of paper. Handing it to him, she said, "This is a phone number where she can be reached."

Thorn glanced at the paper and leaned back in the chair. "She's lost her marbles. That's the only explanation."

Rachel didn't think it was at all crazy to choose to live in Hawaii instead of Bowersville, Iowa, but she didn't think this was the right time to say so. She was happy for Edith, although she hadn't been especially ecstatic at three o'clock that morning.

"It doesn't matter why she's decided to live in Hawaii. Now you have to decide what you're going to do about this house."

"I don't plan on doing anything. She'll be back."

"I'm not so sure. One of the things she asked me to do was contact her bank in Algona to get the deed transferred to you."

Thorn was silent for a long time. Then he said, "I can't believe she's serious about staying in Hawaii."

"And if she is?"

"If she is, then I suppose I'll sell the house."

Rachel pursed her lips, unaware Thorn's gaze was drawn to her mouth. "Ah, it's not going to be that easy."

He tore his gaze from her mouth. "Why not? All I would have to do is get in touch with a real estate agent and put it on the market."

"That's your first problem. There isn't a real estate office in Bowersville. The closest realtor is in Algona."

"So I'll list the house with the realtor in Algona." He saw the way she was frowning. "Why not?"

"I've had the property my grandfather left me listed with the realtor for almost a year. There hasn't been a single nibble on any of the houses or the businesses. Not one. There isn't exactly a rush of people wanting to settle in Bowersville."

Thorn gazed around the large kitchen, remembering the many hours spent there. This room was the center of the house, where his aunt baked her Happy Cookies, canned a wide assortment of vegetables, put up preserves, and always had a glass of milk ready whenever he came home after a day exploring

Bowersville and harassing its citizens. Even though there were five bedrooms, his aunt had decorated a room in the attic for him. It had dormer windows and slanted ceilings with a variety of furniture and mementos stored up there over the years. It was a room where a child's imagination could be given free rein.

The woods behind the house had been Sherwood Forest, a battleground, a fort where he played cowboys and Indians. Once he started college, he hadn't come to Bowersville very often, but he had known it was there.

Yet if he didn't sell the house, what was he going to do with it? If his cuckoo aunt actually carried through with her plans to live in Hawaii, he was going to have to do something about the place. It was too fine a house to be left vacant.

Suddenly restless, he pushed his chair away from the table. "I'm not going to do anything right away. Edith might change her mind again. Lord knows, she's done it enough times the last couple of weeks."

"I'm not so sure," Rachel said doubtfully. "Buying a home in Hawaii sounds fairly permanent."

"I can't imagine selling this place. It just doesn't seem right for Aunt Edith to live anywhere else but here."

Rachel felt she knew what he was going through. She had had mixed feelings about selling her grandfather's property, too, although his house didn't hold all that many fond memories. But now it was hers. It belonged to her. She didn't have many things she could say that about.

She put the cap back onto the thermos. "The

decision about this house is yours. I'm just passing on what Edith told me to tell you."

Thorn had been looking out the window above the sink and turned when he heard her footsteps on the tiled floor. "Where are you going?"

"Home."

"Why?"

Clutching the thermos, she said, "I've told you everything Edith told me."

"Is my aunt the only subject we can talk about?"

"What would you suggest?" She glanced at the window where water was running down the glass. "There's always the weather, of course."

Several long strides brought him within a foot of her. "We could talk about you and me."

"You and me what?"

He took her arm and guided her through the door into the hall. "So far nearly every conversation we've had has been in a kitchen. I'd like a change of scenery."

He led her into the living room. It wasn't the room he wanted to take her to, but for now it was the one he chose. The way she made him feel, the closest bedroom would do just fine. Hell, he thought ruefully, the braided rug in the living room would be just as good. Or the couch.

He took the thermos from her and set it down on one of the end tables. He indicated the stuffed couch. "Have a seat."

Not trusting himself to be too close to her, he chose one of the plump chairs. From experience, he sat down carefully, aware of the broken spring in the bottom cushion. Like all the rest of the furniture, the chair was as old as the house, a good sixty years at least.

He noticed Rachel was aware of the worn condition of the springs in the couch too. She gingerly settled at one end, her legs tucked under her, her weight on the outside of the cushion.

He smiled. "I'm responsible for the broken spring in the couch. I used it as a trampoline once."

"And you broke an antique candy dish and your wrist when you fell off. Edith told me. She also said you got a pip of a spanking after she drove you to Algona to get your wrist put in a cast."

A corner of his mouth twisted into a grimace. "Didn't my aunt ever tell you anything I did right?"

"She did tell me about the time she had a bad cold and you took care of her. Have you always wanted to be a doctor?"

He nodded. "As long as I can remember." He crossed one leg over the other, resting his ankle on his knee. "My father had a small family practice until he died three years ago. He treated everything from skinned knees to heart attacks, delivered babies, and handled any emergency at any hour of the day or night."

"You didn't want a practice like your father's?"

"How do you know I didn't?" Before she could answer, he held up his hand. "Never mind. I know the answer. Aunt Edith. She told you I specialize in sports medicine."

Rachel nodded. "She did mention it. She was impressed by the sight of all those strapping men in your waiting room when she visited you last spring."

"I treat women and children too. She just happened to be there on a day after a rough college ice hockey game where some of the guys got injured."

"Why sports medicine?"

"I've always been interested in sports, so sports medicine seemed a natural specialty. My college roommate specialized in it, too, and he's now my partner. After seeing my father put in fourteen-hour days only to receive a phone call that had him getting out of bed at all hours, I decided against a family practice." He chuckled. "As it turned out, there are emergencies in sports medicine too."

"Edith said you were an only child."

"My mother died when I was young, and my father never remarried. He sent me to his aunt's every summer so I could benefit from a woman's influence. His words, not mine. I also think he wanted a break from fatherhood. It couldn't have been easy for him to be both mother and father."

He tilted his head to one side. "Why all these questions?"

"You said you wanted to talk about you and me. Right now we're talking about you."

"That's not the you and me I meant, and you know it." With a single lithe motion he got out of his chair and walked over to her. His hand closed over her wrist and he pulled her off the couch. "This is what I mean."

Passion exploded between them the moment his mouth covered hers. The raw sound of protest from Rachel conflicted with her sliding her hands around his neck. His tongue plunged past her teeth, tasting, lingering, and tempting her.

Thorn had expected the desire but not the ache, the desperation. The need for her wasn't only physical, although Lord knew that was stronger than anything he had ever experienced. It was deeper, savage, yet tender.

The wanting was easy. It was the longing that was totally different.

Shaken, he slowly drew away from her so he could see her face. "This isn't enough," he said roughly.

Lowering her arms, she spread her fingers out on his chest and let her head rest on his shoulder. Her eyes closed as his scent swirled through her brain, fanning the fires ignited by his kiss. "No," she murmured, her voice muffled but distinct.

She wanted to stay where she was. Pushing against his chest, she shook her head. "It's too much."

He cupped her face in his hands, alarmed to realize they were shaking slightly. "I've never felt anything like this before, Rachel. Not this sudden, not this strong, not ever."

She pulled away from him. "No. It's impossible."

He came after her. With a hand on her arm he turned her to face him. "Don't try to tell me you don't feel something, Rachel. I won't believe you."

"What do you want, Thorn?" she said with spirit, golden lights of anger flashing in her dark eyes. "Does your ego need to hear that I'm attracted to you? Well, I am. I admit it, but I don't fall into bed with men I've known only two days. I'm not going to be used and discarded like yesterday's newspaper when you return to Des Moines. I have more respect for myself than that, even if you don't."

Thorn dropped his hand. She was right, but that didn't stop him from wanting her. He wasn't sure anything could prevent that. It was impossible to think rationally when he ached to feel her under him, when his heated blood raged through him.

Since he didn't argue with her or try to persuade her she was wrong, she stepped around him and walked quickly toward the front door. If she was irrationally disappointed that he didn't attempt to stop her, she would accept it. No matter how long it took.

Within an hour Rachel was back on his front doorstep, pounding on the door. As she drove up the hill to Edith's house, she hadn't known whether he had left for Des Moines. She had been relieved to see his car was still parked in the driveway. Her tires had squealed in protest when she stepped on the brakes, and she had shoved the gear into park before racing to the front door.

She didn't have long to wait. Thorn tore open the door. Sounding like a man who had reached the end of his sanity along with his patience, he growled, "Now what? Have you come to escort me out of town to make sure I leave?"

She shook her head. "There's been an accident at Ruby's Café. There was a grease fire and the cook's been burned. Mrs. Lindstrom slipped on the floor when she went to help the cook put out the fire and hurt her back."

Thorn didn't waste any time asking questions. He disappeared into the house, returning in a few seconds carrying his black medical bag.

"I'll take my car and meet you there."

Rachel nodded. She ran to her car, backed out of the driveway, and sped back to the café.

There were a dozen people clustered around the door of the restaurant and even more inside. As she went around the counter to enter the kitchen, she saw Lars Lindstrom bending over his wife, about to help her up.

"Don't move her, Mr. Lindstrom. Dr. Cannon will be here in a minute. She shouldn't be moved."

The older man reluctantly did as he was told, sitting back on his heels while he held his wife's hand. Several women were with the cook, a middle-aged man who was Mrs. Lindstrom's cousin Jacob. What was left of his apron lay on the floor where it had been flung down and doused with water. Paper towels were spread out on the floor in an attempt to clean up the mess.

A woman had stuck her hand into a bowl of butter and was about to apply it to Jacob's hands and arms.

"Wait!" Rachel said. The woman and Jacob looked at her. "A doctor is on his way. Let's wait until he gets here before we do anything."

The hum of concerned mutterings from the people in the café stilled as Thorn entered. Seeing him, Rachel called out, "Thorn, back here."

He edged around the counter and knelt down next to Mrs. Lindstrom. He asked her a few questions as he examined her, his hands gentle yet thorough as he felt her neck, her arms, and her hips, and flexed her legs. His gaze caught each flinch and pained expression during his examination. Some well-meaning person had put a folded sweater under her head, and he removed it, spreading it over her chest and arms.

In a soft yet authoritative voice he instructed the woman to remain where she was. "Try not to move. I'm going to arrange for an ambulance to take you to the hospital." He saw the fear in the woman's eyes and added, "It's just a precaution. A few X rays and tests."

He patted her arm and smiled down at her as he stood up. He walked over to Rachel. "Where's the nearest hospital?"

"Algona. About thirty miles away."

"Would you call the hospital and arrange for an ambulance to take Mrs. Lindstrom?" He lowered his voice. "Tell them it's a possible spinal injury. Use the phone next door."

She knew why he made the last request. There were a number of curious people within earshot of the pay phone on the wall, including Mrs. Lindstrom and her husband.

The women surrounding the cook moved aside as Thorn approached. He cut the man's sleeves off his shirt, then carefully cleaned off the grease. He asked how the fire had started, more to keep the man's attention off his burns than from a desire to know about the fire.

Rachel returned as he was assuring the cook the burns weren't severe. He wrapped the cook's arms and hands in sterile gauze after applying an ointment. As he began to write a prescription, he told the cook when to apply more ointment and to change the dressing.

Rachel put her hand on his arm, and he looked up.

"Thorn, there isn't a pharmacy in Bowersville."

Agnes Towers and Phyllis Johanneson stepped up immediately. "We'll go to Algona and get the prescription filled for Jacob," Agnes said. Several other people who overheard the conversation also offered to drive to the pharmacy. One of the men volunteered to drive the cook home, and a couple of women said they would bring him his dinner later.

Meanwhile, Mrs. Lindstrom was becoming agitated. With the cook out of commission and herself flat on her back, there was no way the café could stay open. Again her friends and neighbors came forward to offer their assistance. She was not to worry about a thing. Her only concern was to concentrate on getting well.

It was thirty minutes before an ambulance screeched to a halt in front of the café. Thorn supervised the paramedics strapping Mrs. Lindstrom onto a backboard on the stretcher with a cervical collar as a precaution. Mr. Lindstrom accompanied his wife, with a neighbor following the ambulance to the hospital. Several women set about cleaning the kitchen and others served coffee to the people sticking around the café.

Thorn was thumped on the back, thanked numerous times, and had his hand shaken almost continuously as he made his way out of the café. He kept a possessive hold on Rachel's arm while he smiled and accepted the flattering comments by the townspeople. Outside, he was stopped several times more, but was finally able to walk Rachel to her car.

She saw the bemused expression on his face as he stared back at the people who had just thanked him profusely. "Medical care is scarce in Bowersville," she explained. "Everyone appreciates what you did."

He brought his gaze back to her. "Do the people rally around each other like that all the time?"

She nodded. "They're like the Three Musketeers.

All for one and one for all. It's a way of life to these people, as natural as breathing."

Thorn still looked preoccupied as he opened her door for her. Rachel hesitated before getting in her car. She held out her hand. "I suppose you'll be leaving now, so I'll say good-bye and add my thanks to all the rest. I was next door at Peabody's when I heard about the accident at Ruby's. I immediately thought of you. I hope you don't mind that I asked you to help."

He looked down at her hand but didn't take it. "I'm surprised you thought about me at all, even if it was only as a doctor rather than as a man."

Lowering her hand, Rachel turned away so he couldn't see how his harsh words hurt her. It was just as well he didn't know how often she had thought about him during the last few days.

Thorn's gaze remained on her car as she drove away. He didn't know why he had said that. The only excuse he had was that so much had happened during the last couple of days, he was considerably off balance. His usual calm, analytical mind seemed to have taken a vacation. But not his desire for Rachel.

He had a feeling that wasn't going to go away.

Suddenly he made a decision. He wasn't going to go away either.

Five

An hour later Rachel was in her studio when the phone rang. At first she was going to ignore it, but when it kept on ringing, she finally got off the stool and answered it.

Expecting it to be her persistent agent, she said, "I'll save you some time, Henry. The answer is no."

"Who's Henry?" a deep voice demanded.

"Thorn? I thought you'd left."

"Who's Henry?"

"Never mind Henry. Why are you calling?"

"I want you to get your sweet little tush over here. This is all your fault."

Rachel started to ask him what in blue blazes he was talking about, but she didn't get a chance. He had hung up.

There hadn't been time for him to drive back to Des Moines, so he was obviously still in town. She should just ignore him, she told herself. She really should. They had already said good-bye. At least she had. There wasn't anything left to say. If she had any sense at all, she would return to her drawing table and work on her strip. So why was she cleaning her pens, she wondered with irritation. Maybe it was his statement about something being all her fault. Or possibly even his inelegant command. She could convince herself it was for a variety of reasons. Most of them would be wrong.

She sighed heavily. She was going because she couldn't do anything else.

When she arrived there were several cars parked in front of Edith's house, and a woman holding a baby was approaching the front door. When Rachel came up the walk, the woman turned and smiled.

"Hello, Rachel."

"Hi, Sarah." Through the open door Rachel could see others inside. "What's going on?"

"I'm bringing Dr. Cannon a tunafish casserole. Isn't it wonderful we have a doctor in town? We don't have to go all the way to Algona every time one of the kids gets sick or breaks a bone."

Now Rachel knew what Thorn had meant when he said it was all her fault. Because of her taking him to the café to help Mrs. Lindstrom and her cook, the whole community knew there was a doctor in town.

"Sarah, Dr. Cannon doesn't plan on staying in Bowersville. He lives in Des Moines. He's here only for the weekend."

The other woman looked crestfallen. "Are you sure? Gladys Olson told me Edith's nephew was staying at her house and had saved Mrs. Lindstrom's life. She said he treated Jacob for some real bad burns and Jacob's doing fine now."

Rachel groaned inwardly. Oh, boy, she thought. Things were getting out of hand. She followed Sarah into the house, where they were greeted by Gladys Olson and her sister, Velma. Velma took the casserole from Sarah and led the way into the dining room. The women chatted away in their usual friendly fashion, clearly excited by the new arrival in town.

Velma put Sarah's casserole on the dining room table, pushing several other foil-wrapped dishes aside to make room for it. There was enough food on the table to feed a family of four for a month.

Other people were standing around in the dining room, but there was no sign of Thorn. Turning to Gladys, Rachel asked, "Where's Dr. Cannon?"

"I believe he's in the study, dear. He said he had a phone call to make."

Rachel didn't bother knocking on the closed door. She slid into the study and closed the door behind her. Thorn was seated at his aunt's antique desk with the phone held to his ear. The moment he saw her, he slammed the phone down.

"It's about time you got here," he said, getting out of the chair and striding around the desk. "I was just trying to phone you again." He took her arms and held her in front of him. "Rachel, there are hordes of little old ladies coming out of the woodwork."

She chuckled. "You make it sound like you're being attacked by fire ants. I should have realized how everyone would react to having a doctor in town, if only temporarily. I was thinking only of getting help for Mrs. Lindstrom and Jacob when I came to get you."

"I called the hospital and talked to the doctor who examined Mrs. Lindstrom. She's sprained a few muscles in her back, but there's no damage to her spine. She has to have bedrest for a week or two before she returns to the café."

He could have told her that on the phone, Rachel thought. "That's good news."

Thorn leaned back against the desk, half-sitting on the edge, bringing her along with him. Parting his legs, he moved her between them, ignoring her stiffness as she resisted the intimate contact. She was going to have to get used to being close to him, he thought.

Keeping his voice even and casual, he asked, "Who's Henry?"

She had the feeling he wouldn't be satisfied until she answered his question. "He's my agent."

"You need an agent for a comic strip?"

"It helps."

He searched her eyes, his expression serious. "You don't give away much about yourself, do you? I can't decide whether you're intensely private or you have something to hide. You drop tidbits of information as miserly as Scrooge drops pennies."

"My grandfather wasn't the type of man who encouraged conversations, much less confidences. Maybe that's why I've always had difficulty talking about myself. He once said he didn't expect anyone else to take care of his problems, and I shouldn't expect him to take care of mine. I've been in the habit of taking care of my own problems and minding my own business for a long time. Which reminds me, why did you call me to come over here?"

He accepted the change of subject. She had given

him a few more pieces. He wanted all of them, but there were other pressing matters to deal with at the moment. Like a houseful of people.

"You're the expert on this town. What am I supposed to do with all those people out there?"

To keep her balance when he had pulled her between his legs, she had automatically placed her hands on his thighs. Her fingers slowly stroked the firm muscles until she realized what she was doing. She snatched her hands away, and it took her a minute to remember the question he had asked. Her voice was oddly breathless as she answered, "All you have to do is explain you have to leave for Des Moines."

A small smile played at a corner of his mouth as he looked down at her. "I can't do that."

"Why not?"

"Because I'm staying."

"No, you're not."

He chuckled. "Yes, I am."

"But you can't."

"Why not?" he asked, his hands settling on her hips with an easy intimacy that shook her.

She frowned at him. The reasons were so obvious, she felt foolish pointing them out to him. "You have your practice in Des Moines."

"I also have a partner. In a way, this was his idea, although I've modified his suggestion somewhat." She looked thoroughly bewildered. "I called Richard earlier. He's taking over my patients for a while."

Her next question was laced with wariness. "How long is a while?"

Sliding his hands around her waist and clasping

them behind her, he held her loosely. "As long as it takes," he said cryptically.

"You're not making any sense, Thorn."

"I'm not surprised. I seem to have lost my senses after entering the town limits of Bowersville."

"Then perhaps it would be better if you left the town limits and went back to Des Moines. Think of all those jocks who need your expertise."

His fingers spread out over the slender bones of her hips. "Is that what you want?"

Being so close to him wasn't making it easy for her to think about anything but him. "What I want isn't the issue."

"Yes, it is." He gave in to the need to feel her mouth under his and lowered his head. Against her lips he said quietly, "This is what we both want."

Deliberate male hunger met a natural feminine response. It would be easier to cease breathing than to stop the desire from flowing between them. Blood heated, breathing quickened, and flesh craved flesh.

Rachel absorbed the taste of him, the feel of his strength against her softness. With a desperation sparked by knowing he would be leaving soon no matter what he said, she gave to him fully. This would be the last time she could experience the magic only Thorn could create within her.

A sharp rap on the wooden door broke the spell of sensuality. An elderly female voice called out, "Dr. Cannon?"

Without releasing Rachel, he drew his head back and answered. "Yes?"

"There's a woman here who needs to talk to you for a moment."

"I'll be right out."

He looked down at Rachel. "Will you stay? We need to talk."

"Thorn . . ."

He shook his head. "I've made a few decisions. Since some of them involve you, you have a right to know what they are."

She stood back as he gently put her from him. Feeling suddenly cold when he withdrew his warmth, she wrapped her arms around herself.

Mrs. McPherson was waiting patiently near the door and took his arm to draw him away with her. Seeing Rachel, Mrs. McPherson smiled and said, "Rachel, why don't you help the ladies put away the food in the kitchen? That way you and Dr. Cannon will know where everything is when you want to eat something."

Rachel wasn't ready to face the fine citizens of Bowersville yet, but she didn't have much choice. Nor could she do anything about Mrs. McPherson's assumption she would be dining with Thorn. Apparently the rest of the townspeople had them paired off already. Protesting or attempting to explain would only make matters more complicated.

Rachel left the study and walked toward the dining room. They would all know there was nothing between her and Thorn once he returned to Des Moines and she stayed behind.

The sun was beginning to set as the last friendly citizen shook Thorn's hand and departed. The phone had finally stopped ringing, and he was able to shut the door and lock it.

Leaning against the door for a moment, he took a

deep breath, then pushed himself away. After looking in the study and the living room, he walked toward the kitchen.

Expecting to see Rachel, he frowned when he found the kitchen dark. He turned on the light and looked around. There were still a few containers of food on the table. Apparently there hadn't been enough room in the refrigerator. Then he noticed the back door was ajar. Someone had evidently set something out on the back porch and forgot to shut the door. Remembering the crowded condition of that porch, he wondered where they had found room to put anything.

Slowly he walked over to the door, feeling disappointed that Rachel had left. But he told himself he shouldn't be surprised after what he had said to her in the study. He knew he was rushing her, yet the way he was feeling, it wasn't fast enough.

As he placed his hand on the latch of the door, he saw a movement in the shadows of the porch. "Rachel?"

Her soft answer came from the dimly lit interior. "Yes."

Relief washed over him in waves. Stepping around a wobbly table, he said, "What are you doing out here?"

"I was watching the sun set."

"Why don't you come back inside? We can find out what's in some of the wrapped dishes those ladies brought over. I haven't eaten today."

She continued to look out at the fading sun. "I'm not hungry. You go ahead."

The toe of his shoe bumped into a carton of empty canning jars, setting them rattling against each other.

"What's all this stuff? This is a hazard to life and limb."

"Your aunt doesn't like to throw anything away. I think that's one of the reasons she understood my grandfather. He kept everything too. Your aunt places a close second in the pack-rat category." She turned to look at him. "I can recommend a good trucking firm when you're ready."

"When I'm ready for what?" He quickly grabbed a coat rack that started to tip over when he bumped it with his elbow. "Why would I want a trucking firm?"

"You said you'd made some decisions. I figured the selling of this house was one of them. When you do sell it, you'll have to take care of the contents somehow. There are a couple of small items Edith wants sent to Hawaii, like the antique clock in the living room and her silver. There are a few other things, but I can't remember offhand. I wrote them down when she called. The rest she said is yours to do with as you wish."

When she started to list some antique dealers in the neighboring town he might want to contact, he took matters in his own hands. Literally.

Taking her arm, he began to lead her carefully around the clutter on the porch toward the kitchen. "This house is one of the things I want to talk about. But not here." His head collided with a tin watering can that was hanging from a hook.

Rachel heard him mumble a colorful word under his breath. "Are you all right?"

"I'm peachy keen, thanks," he said dryly.

Even though it wasn't funny he had hit his head, she found herself smiling. His humor, his ability to laugh at himself, was one of the things she liked about him. And the number of those things was growing.

Once they were safely in the kitchen, Thorn opened the refrigerator. He peeked under the foil of several of the covered dishes, then removed two and placed them on the counter.

"There's a kerosene lamp on a shelf in the pantry. If you'll carry it, I'll get the rest."

She didn't move. "The rest of what?"

He had returned to the refrigerator. His arms were full when he turned around. Taking a cardboard box off the floor, he put the dishes inside. "You've told me about your tree house. Now I'll show you one of my favorite places."

"Thorn," she began hesitantly. "I . . ."

He stopped what he was doing and looked at her. "I know. You're not hungry and you want to go home. Putting me off isn't going to change anything, Rachel."

It was irritating that he knew what she was thinking, what she had been about to say. She might as well get it over with tonight, she decided, rather than postpone their chat to another time.

"I'll get the lamp," she murmured with little enthusiasm.

Thorn gave her one last long look. She didn't like it, but she was going to stay.

After gathering everything he wanted, he led the way through the back porch out into the yard. The only sounds were being made by crickets conducting their nightly serenade. Thorn took her hand as they walked across the grass. He didn't seem to need the light from the lamp, but Rachel held it out in front of her anyway.

In a corner of Edith's property was a large weeping willow, and this was Thorn's destination. He took the lamp and held some of the branches out of the way for her. Following her, he set the lamp on the grass before he spread out a large rug and knelt down on it. Moving the lamp to the center of the rug, he began to empty the contents of the box.

Rachel looked around. "So this is your secret place?"

"Yup. What do you think of it?"

"I like it." She joined him on the rug. "It has all the comforts of home."

Thorn could have made a comment about it being as furnished as her own home was, but he didn't. "You're the first person I ever invited here. I hope you feel suitably honored."

"Oh, I do," she said lightly. She drew her legs up and wrapped her arms around them. "What did you do when you came here?"

He took out a bottle of Edith's homemade dandelion wine and held it up. "One day I snuck a bottle of this stuff Edith affectionately calls wine. I drank the whole thing while perusing a choice collection of girlie magazines."

She smiled. "How decadent."

The cork popped. "I was eleven or twelve at the time, not smart enough to know that a whole bottle of this stuff could stunt my growth. After the bottle was empty, I fell asleep." He gestured toward the trunk of the tree. "Right over there. It started to rain, and I was so out of it, I didn't even notice. The rain ruined my magazines. I also had a hangover to beat all hangovers the next day."

"It sounds like you were more distressed at having your magazines ruined than having a hangover."

"They were extremely educational at that point in my life."

"I bet they were. Did Edith know you had dived into one of her batches of wine?"

He nodded as he poured wine into two glasses. "She thought it was funny." Handing her one of the glasses, he saw the amusement in her eyes. "So do you, I see."

Rachel chuckled. "It is funny."

"I didn't think so at the time." Lifting his glass in a toast, he said quietly, "To my secret place, and now yours."

The hanging branches and the darkness outside created an intimate leafy cave. There was little breeze and the leaves hung motionless in the light of the lamp. It was as though they were in their own private world.

"Dr. Cannon," she said softly, "I do believe you are a romantic at heart."

He placed a leg of chicken on a paper plate. "I'm not ashamed to admit it. I'm a sucker for soft light, soft music, and a soft companion. Tonight I've got two out of three."

"I could hum a few bars of 'Moonlight Becomes You' if you like."

Chuckling, he continued dishing out their meal. "I think we can do without the music tonight. Maybe another time."

He began to load her plate with chicken, potato salad, and macaroni salad. Pausing for a moment, he asked, "Do you want the green jiggly stuff or the pink wiggly stuff? I'm not sure what either one is, but one has fruit in it and the other cottage cheese. I think."

"Neither one, thanks." Her eyes widened as she looked at the plate he handed her. "Good Lord, Thorn. I can't possibly eat all this."

"Try to eat some of it. Those ladies brought enough food for the National Guard." He frowned. "You aren't one of those women who are always on a diet, are you?"

She thought she detected a hint of disapproval in his voice. Smiling faintly, she shook her head. "Food isn't one of my priorities, that's all."

"What is your priority?"

She picked up a piece of chicken and set the plate down on the rug. " 'Fancy Fannie.' I've wanted my own strip for a long time. Now the challenge is to keep it going, to come up with fresh ideas."

"And that's enough for you? Have you ever heard the old saying about all work and no play? Don't you feel any need to have more in your life than work?"

"I'm not working now."

His smile was warm and intimate. "No. You're not, are you? Tell me about your most romantic evening. Does this compare favorably or unfavorably?"

Her mouth twisted ruefully. "There haven't been all that many."

He made a sound of disbelief. "You're kidding."

"No. I attended an all-girl school, which didn't exactly give me a lot of experience with the male sex."

"Rachel," he said patiently, "I hope you aren't going to expect me to believe you didn't date after you left school."

Since she couldn't think of a graceful way out of

this conversation, she had no choice but to continue. "My grandfather was the antisocial member of the family. Not me."

He shook his head. "You have a marvelous way of answering a question without actually saying anything. It could become really irritating if you keep it up."

He had expected her to clam up completely then, but instead she laughed. "Your questions aren't exactly obvious either. Why don't you come right out and ask me about the men in my life?"

"I did."

"In a roundabout way."

He grinned. "That's only fair. That's how you answered me." He held up his hand when she opened her mouth to speak. "Let's try it again. Tell me about the men in your life. Past, present, and future."

The slender branches of the willow tree swayed around them in response to a gust of wind. Lifting her hand to brush away one of the long, frail boughs, she said, "In the past there was only one serious relationship. It didn't work out. At present I'm having a picnic with you. As to the future, like everyone else I have to wait to see what it will bring."

He honed in on the brief statement she had made about her past. "Why didn't the previous relationship work out?"

She scowled at him. "You are one persistent man."

"True. Do you want me to repeat the question?"

"No," she said with resignation. "The simplest answer is that he couldn't accept the fact that I wanted a career of my own. I couldn't accept not having a career." She paused, then added, "Is the inquisition over?"

"For now."

His gaze roamed over her, lingering on the tantalizing swell of her breasts and settling on her face. The glow from the lamp was highlighting the golden lights in her dark eyes. He had brought her out to the willow tree on impulse. Now he could see it had been a wise move. She was more relaxed than she had ever been with him.

Changing the subject, she asked, "What did you want to talk to me about? You said something about having made some decisions."

He took a sip of wine and grimaced at the taste. "Yuck. No matter how many batches of the stuff Edith makes, her wine never improves. It tastes like old salad dressing." Clearing his throat, he continued. "You were right. Edith doesn't plan on coming back."

Rachel stared at him. "What's made you change your mind? You didn't believe me before."

"I called the number you gave me. Taylor Mead answered, and I talked to him first." He gave her a pained smile. "You were also right about him. He seems to be a nice enough guy. Apparently he's learned how to manage his new wife already. She wanted to take instructions in skin diving, but he talked her into taking hula lessons instead."

Rachel choked back a laugh. "And you were worried about her. It sounds like she's having the time of her life."

"I still think she's making some fairly radical changes in her life for a woman of her age, but she sounded happy when I talked to her." Sprawling out on the rug beside her, he propped himself up on an elbow. "In fact, she was downright ecstatic. Would you like to know why?"

Rachel looked down at him. All she had to do was move her hand eight inches, and she would be able to smooth back the lock of dark hair that had fallen onto his forehead. To keep from reaching out to touch him, she nibbled on some chicken.

"Aside from the fact," she said after a moment, her tone dry, "that Edith just got married and is going to be living in paradise, I can't imagine why she could possibly be ecstatic."

Thorn's gaze remained locked on her face. "You didn't know what she was doing, did you?"

"What are you talking about? Of course I know what she's been doing. I was the one she phoned at three in the morning so she could tell me she was going to stay in Hawaii. Remember?"

"My dearly beloved aunt set us up, Rachel," he drawled. "You and me and she's hoping baby will make three."

Rachel's mouth dropped open. She wouldn't have been able to speak even if her life depended on it. She was having enough trouble simply breathing. The implication of what he had said was too over-whelming to take in right away.

If he had hauled off and struck her, Thorn didn't think Rachel would be as stunned as she was now. He reached over and closed her mouth by placing a finger under her jaw. His thumb brushed across her bottom lip before he dropped his hand.

"It was somewhat of a shock to me too," he said. "Also a relief. The one thing I couldn't understand was how she could get married without letting me

To get a free *Loveswept* ® calendar, packed with information about *Loveswept* romances in 1990, simply fill out the form below.

Calendar available early December, 1989. Offer good while supplies last.

Name _____

Address _____

City _____ State _____ Zip _____

Would you please give us the following information:

Did you buy Loveswept Golden Classics (on sale in June)?
____Yes ____No

If your answer is yes, did you buy __1 __2 __3 __4

Will you buy Golden Classics featuring Hometown Hunks on the covers?
I will buy 1-2____, 3-4 ____, All 6____ None____

How often would you like to have an opportunity to purchase Golden Classics?
Every month_____ If so, how many per month_____
Quarterly_____

* One calendar per household.

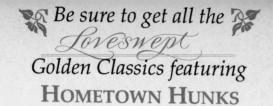

Be sure to get all the

Loveswept

Golden Classics featuring

HOMETOWN HUNKS

On sale in October

BUSINESS REPLY MAIL

FIRST-CLASS MAIL   PERMIT NO. 174   NEW YORK, NY

Postage will be paid by addressee

Loveswept

Bantam Books
Dept. CN
666 Fifth Avenue
New York, NY 10103

NO POSTAGE
NECESSARY
IF MAILED
IN THE
UNITED STATES

know beforehand. It really bothered me. It's why I thought something was wrong."

"What—" she started huskily, and cleared her throat before trying again. "What did Edith say?"

He didn't touch her. He wanted to, but this wasn't the time. She would have to hear the news cold turkey. As he had.

"My sweet sainted aunt decided one way to get me to come to Bowersville was to send me a cryptic postcard announcing her marriage as an accomplished fact. It worked. As soon as I got the card, I came to Bowersville, seeking some answers."

"I don't understand. Why did she want you to come to Bowersville if she wasn't here?"

He watched her carefully to see her reaction. "You were here."

Comprehension came slowly, and when it did, she could only stare at him as though he had lost his mind. "You can't mean she wanted us to . . ."

When her voice trailed off, he nodded and finished what she was going to say. "Become involved. That's what the lady wanted, and that's what she got."

Rachel sprang up off the rug. Backing away from him, she denied everything he said. "No. We aren't involved. I don't care what warped plot Edith's concocted. You are going back to Des Moines to put casts on broken legs, and I'm staying here to continue with my own life. She's just going to have to be disappointed."

In a quick movement Thorn got to his feet. "She's not the only one," he murmured as he came after her.

He drew her away from the willow branches back to the rug. Kneeling in front of her, he took both her hands in his and tugged on them until she, too, was on her knees in front of him. She stiffened at his touch, but he no longer resented it. He expected it.

"We are involved, Rachel." When she started to shake her head, he cupped her face. "You can protest all you want, but it won't make any difference. If you're angry, say so. If you think I'm wrong about us, if you want me to get the hell out of your life, you'll have to come right out and say so. But don't try to tell me we aren't involved."

She was tempted to tell him to go, to get out of her life. It would be the easy way. A simple renunciation of her feelings. Without her realizing it was happening, her fingers curled around his, holding on to him even as she thought of letting him go.

"I can't," she admitted, making it sound like a guilty confession as she lowered her head.

Thorn's arms went around her as tenderness welled up inside him. "Which can't you do?" he asked softly. "You can't get angry or you can't tell me to get the hell out of your life?"

Her voice was muffled as she spoke. "Yes."

"Yes what?" he prompted her, not satisfied with her answer, needing to hear the words from her, knowing she needed to say them.

She raised her head. Temper glinted in her eyes. She clutched a handful of his shirtfront tightly. "You're going to see me damn angry in a minute. Stop pushing."

"Tell me what you want," he said gently, unaffected by her temper. "You already know what I want."

Her fingers loosened their grip, but she didn't move away. "If you had asked me three days ago, I could have given you an answer." She took a deep breath and met his intent gaze. "You confuse me, you irritate me, you disturb me, and you push me into so many directions, I don't know which way I'm going. One minute I wish you had never come to Bowersville, and the next minute I'm afraid you'll leave."

Was there ever going to be a time when she didn't surprise him, he wondered. He had gotten more than he had asked for. Placing his hands on either side of her face, he looked down at her. Whether she realized it or not, she had told him more than she thought she had.

She hadn't finished. "Thorn, why are you staying?"

He studied her. She might not be ready to hear it, but he was ready to say it. "There are a number of reasons. There's this house. That's part of it. There are also the people at the café and those who came here today. It might sound strange, but I felt what I did for the cook and Mrs. Lindstrom was why I became a doctor. The thanks I received from the townspeople was more valuable than any amount of money. What I did for those people was appreciated and important to every single person in the town."

Rachel unconsciously stroked his chest. "I'm sure what you do for your patients in Des Moines is appreciated too."

He shrugged. "Maybe, but I've never felt so good about practicing medicine as I have now. Helping those people was more satisfying than money or prestige." He covered her hand with one of his. "The main reason I'm staying is I need time to figure out what the hell is happening between us."

"Nothing is happening between us," she said with feeling, denying what he was saying.

Still holding her hand in his, he brushed his knuckles against her breast, his gaze on her eyes. "Isn't there?"

"I . . . Dammit, Thorn. Don't."

"How long do you think you'll need before you'll know one way or the other?"

She shook her head. "I don't know."

"Perhaps this will help you."

He slowly lowered her to the rug, coming down with her. She was still holding on to the front of his shirt, as if it were a lifeline. In a way it was. He was. She had never felt as though she were drowning just by looking into a man's eyes. •

For a moment he simply gazed down at her. Then he lowered his head. His mouth was firm yet coaxing as he pried her lips apart. Her fingers clenched, then spread out over his chest, a soft moan of pleasure and completion coming from deep within her.

Tenderness merged with desire. Needs rose to meet hunger. Hands stroked flesh, creating a deeper craving with each caress.

He unbuttoned her shirt, exposing the black silk chemise she wore underneath. Her outer clothing was ordinary, he thought but there was nothing average or common about what she wore beneath. He shifted to one side, allowing the light from the lamp to flow over her.

"You're very beautiful, Rachel." His hand skimmed across her rib cage and cupped her breast. He heard her quick intake of breath and saw the startled expression in her eyes.

She clasped his wrist in an attempt to stop him

from going any further. "Thorn, the neighbors. They can see us."

His thumb lightly caressed the tip into a hard bud. "Mr. Grundy is the only close neighbor, and the shades are pulled down at his windows. He couldn't care less about our secret place. There's just you and me."

She didn't look reassured. As he gazed down at her, he was puzzled by the expression in her eyes. Desire he expected, but not uncertainty. Or was it fear, he wondered. A sudden thought occurred to him. It was hard to believe. It was also impossible to understand, but every instinct inside him told him he was right. If he was, it explained why she reacted as she did when he touched her.

"Rachel," he murmured softly, "have you ever been with a man before?"

Six

She wanted to look away, but she didn't. Meeting his gaze, she asked, "Would it make a difference?"

His voice was harsher than he intended. "If you have to ask that question, you've just answered mine."

Withdrawing his hand from her breast, he pulled the edges of her shirt together to cover her. Stopping from making love with her was the hardest thing he had ever had to do. His hands shook slightly as he started to button her shirt, aware of her puzzled gaze.

Abruptly he sat up, pulling his legs up and resting his head on his knees. Passion still beat heavily in his blood, and he needed time to cool down. And time to think.

Just when he was so sure he knew where he stood, she knocked him off his feet.

"Give me a minute," he said, his voice muffled, "and then I'll take you home."

Rachel remained where she was, staring up at the

shadowy branches of the tree overhead. A moment ago she had felt as though she were doused in fire, and now she couldn't feel anything. Her arms were oddly heavy as she raised them to finish buttoning her shirt. As she sat up, she watched her fingers maneuver each button through the buttonhole as though it were the most important thing she'd ever done.

For the first time in her life she had been willing to open herself up to another person. And he had turned his back on her. Pride stiffened her spine and her determination. It wouldn't happen again. She should have known better than to let things go as far as they had.

Without making a sound she stood and silently pushed back the curtain of willow branches behind Thorn. There was enough light filtering through the foliage for her to see where she was walking until she was on more familiar ground near Edith's house.

Thorn couldn't believe he had actually been sitting on Rachel's front steps for two hours. He hadn't been completely alone. Every mosquito in Bowersville was keeping him company.

He should go back to his aunt's house. Swatting his neck, he corrected that thought. He should get in his car and head back to Des Moines, where he knew what he was doing, where he knew what each day would bring. The trouble was, this was where Rachel was. Or at least where she was supposed to be.

Her car was gone. She could be anywhere and come home anytime. There was the off chance she wouldn't return, but he didn't want to think about that. If necessary, he would stay on her doorstep all night. Underneath his impatience ran a thin line of anger. Earlier that evening, when he had turned around and found she had slipped away, his first reaction had been frustrated fury. She was just so damn elusive, like smoke drifting through his fingers.

For about the twentieth time since he had taken up his vigil, he wondered why he kept coming back when she made it clear she didn't want to be involved with him. What he couldn't understand was why she held him off. She was as aware as he of the attraction between them. She might not want to acknowledge it, but she couldn't deny the desire that flared whenever they were together.

It was too late for him. After the second day he had gone past the point of no return and wanted only to go forward, the destination as yet unknown. What he was sure of was how badly he wanted her to be with him while they found out where they were headed.

When it began to rain, he moved off the steps and sheltered under the overhanging porch. He pulled up the collar of his lightweight jacket and leaned his shoulder against the front door. The porch roof leaked in a number of places, but he'd stay relatively dry as long as he stood near the door.

He shook his head in bemusement. Only an idiot would do what he was doing. A man who had lost his mind. Or his heart.

Finally his vigil paid off when he sighted a pair of headlights on the narrow road. He stayed in the shadows as Rachel's car turned into the wide driveway and stopped beside his. Lightning illuminated the area briefly, and he saw her staring through her windshield at his car.

The muscles in his stomach knotted as he waited to see what she would do. Minutes passed. The rain was coming down in sheets, accompanied by lightning and thunder. Rachel remained in the car. She could be waiting for the rain to let up before getting out, but his store of patience had been used up.

By the time he reached her car, his hair and shoulders were soaked thoroughly. He yanked open her door and pulled her out into the rain, slamming the door shut once she was standing in front of him.

"Where in hell have you been?"

Rachel blinked, shocked at the violence in his voice. "I drove to Algona."

"Why?"

"To mail a week's supply of strips."

"At this hour? The post office is closed."

"I know how much postage it takes. I put the stamps on myself before I left. On the way back, I stopped at the Thompsons' place to talk to Tony today instead of tomorrow."

His fingers closed around her arms, and he practically lifted her off the ground so her eyes were level with his. "Don't ever do that to me again. I . . . oh, hell!"

His last words were said against her mouth just before he crushed her lips under his own. The elements of nature were calm compared to the storm of passion engulfing them. Desperation and hunger melded with need as Thorn's arms tightened around her slender body. His mouth slanted over hers, deepening the assault on her lips. Their wet clothing quickly became plastered to their bodies, but neither of them noticed.

A loud crash of thunder brought Thorn back to reality. He became aware of water running down his face and soaking their clothing. Lifting his head, he gazed at her dripping hair and rain-slick face.

"Dammit, Rachel," he murmured huskily. "I've been worried about you."

She was startled. Not only because he had been concerned about her but because her arms were wrapped around his neck. She didn't remember putting them there.

Loosening her hold on him, she said, "I'm fine."

Frustration rasped against relief. "Why did you leave? I turned around and you had vanished. Why?"

"You made your point when you turned your back on me tonight. You wanted an experienced woman, and I'm not."

His arms tightened when she began to draw away. "Rachel, I needed a little time to cool down. Wanting you isn't something I can turn off like I would a light switch." His hands slid over her hips, dragging her lower body against him, showing her how she affected him. "It's not something I can control, but I can control what I do about it. I was trying to do the right thing. Your first time with a man should be special, not a rough coupling under a tree."

"It would have been special with you."

Her quiet statement stunned him, and all he could do was stare at her.

A loud clap of thunder made Rachel's body jerk against his. Thorn took her hand. "Let's go inside before we get washed away." He ran toward the house, dragging her along with him. When they were on the porch, he asked, "Where's your key?"

Catching her breath, she said, "The door isn't locked."

Thorn choked back a laugh. "I waited for hours outside being eaten alive by bloodthirsty mosquitoes and getting dripped on by your leaky porch roof, when I could have been inside where it was mosquitoless and dry?" Without giving her an opportunity to answer, he asked, "Why don't you lock your doors?"

"It might have escaped your notice, but there isn't a lot to steal."

"Aside from the fact you're a woman living alone, you have a lot of valuable art equipment in your studio."

"Bowersville isn't exactly the crime capital of the state. I could have the Crown Jewels here and they would be safe." She opened the door and stepped inside.

"I'm more concerned about you than your possessions," he said. A flash of bright lightning allowed him to see the same startled look she had given him earlier. "Why are you so surprised that I was worried about you?"

Because being worried about her meant he cared, she thought, and she found it hard to believe he could care about her so quickly. She gave him a faint smile. "I'm not accustomed to having anyone worrying about me." She flicked the light switch several times without any results. "Oh, great. The storm has knocked out the lights."

"I have a flashlight in my car."

"There's no need for you to go out in the rain again. I have some candles in the kitchen." She paused before adding, "If you'd rather go back to Edith's, I'll be all right here on my own. This isn't the first time the lights have gone out."

He couldn't see her expression in the darkness.

"I'm not leaving, Rachel," he said solemnly. "Not until we get a few things straightened out."

There was only the sound of the rain pelting down on the windows. "All right," she finally said. "You stay there while I get the candles. I know my way around the house better than you do."

He couldn't argue with that. There wasn't any furniture to bump into, but there were solid walls. While he waited for her to return he shrugged out of his jacket and tossed it over the newel post of the stairs. He saw the glow from the candles before he saw Rachel. When she came into view, his breath caught in his throat. By daylight she was beautiful. By candlelight she literally took his breath away.

She handed him one of the candles. Instead of going back to the kitchen as he expected, she walked toward the stairs. He followed her up and into the bathroom off the landing. In the flickering candle-light he could make out the old-fashioned claw-footed tub and the partially tiled walls. There was a single window above the tub, covered by peach-colored cur-tains that matched the small flowers in the soft gray wallpaper above the tiles. Peach towels hung from porcelain towel racks. The wallpaper looked new and definitely not something Old Man Baskin would have chosen.

Rachel set her candle down on the counter near the sink and opened a cupboard built into the wall. She handed him a thick towel and took one for herself, wiping the moisture off her face and rub-bing her hair. There was nothing that could be done about their soaked clothing except to remove it.

"Obviously my clothes dryer isn't going to work," she said. "I could turn on the oven and drape your clothes over a chair in front of the open door to dry them. But I don't have anything for you to wear in the meantime."

He found her uncertainty oddly endearing. It was obvious she had never been in this situation before and was at a loss what to do about it. She might feel comfortable dressing in front of him, as she had that day by the river, but she wasn't used to men being undressed. He couldn't help being pleased with that thought.

"You go change," he said. "I'll find something."

She nodded and left the bathroom, shutting the door behind her. After setting her candle in its pewter holder on the antique dresser in her bedroom, she rummaged through a drawer for dry underclothing. If she had been alone, she would have slipped on her robe. Instead, she pulled from her closet a pair of peach broadcloth slacks with a matching long sleeved safari-style shirt. She rolled up the sleeves several turns before adding a belt around her waist.

She was running her fingers through her drying hair when the bathroom door opened and Thorn strolled out, wearing a towel draped around his hips. In one hand he carried his sodden clothing. He held the candle up in the other.

His mouth went dry when he caught sight of her wildly mussed hair. His gaze shifted to her slender figure dressed in the casual slacks and shirt. Smiling faintly he said, "If I've ever seen a more beautiful, desirable woman than you, I can't think of when."

She saw the heat flaring in his eyes. "Thorn . . ."

"Here are my clothes. I hope they dry fast because we'll both feel safer with clothes between us."

She knew why *she* would feel safer if he was fully dressed, but she wondered why *he* would. Picking up her candle, she took his clothes and left her bedroom. As she went down the stairs, she realized he was remaining in her room instead of coming with her.

Holding his candle up, Thorn looked around her bedroom. All the furniture had been built at least a hundred years ago. The double bed had an ornately carved headboard and was covered with an antique quilt done in a variety of materials in shades of blue and white. A rocking chair occupied a corner of the room with a small table next to it. On the table was a book with a tasseled bookmark stuck about halfway through. He picked up the book, curious about what she read. In gold-stamped letters imprinted on the ancient leather binding, he read: Little Dorritt by Charles Dickens. A classy lady reads the classics.

Replacing the book, he looked over at the recessed window seat covered with blue fabric that matched the plump pillows propped up at each end. Several other books were stacked on the cushion. A single watercolor painting hung on one wall between the rocking chair and a tall chest of drawers. On a nightstand next to the bed a telephone sat next to a clock radio.

Thorn walked over to the dresser and examined the objects on its polished surface, hoping to find some sort of clue to help him unravel the complex puzzle of Rachel Hyatt. Aside from a jewelry chest and two bottles of perfume, there were no other personal items, no framed pictures of family members or friends.

When he heard a board creak in the hall, he turned toward the doorway in time to see Rachel enter, carrying a tray. On the tray were her candle, two cups, and a pot of coffee. She set the tray on the dresser and poured out the hot coffee.

Handing him a cup, she said, "I thought this might help keep you warm until your clothes are dry."

His temperature had gone up several degrees when she had entered the room. He accepted the cup and said, "Thanks." Glancing around the room, he added, "Your room surprises me."

She smiled. "Why? Because it has furniture?"

"Compared to the rest of the house, it was a shock to see an actual chair, much less a bed."

He watched her carry her cup over to the rocking chair and sit down, one leg curled under her. Feeling too restless to sit, especially on her bed, he walked over to the window. He was unable to see anything beyond the rain-splattered pane, and focused his attention on the water trickling down the glass.

"Rachel, why haven't you furnished the house other than the kitchen, your studio, and your bedroom?"

Thorn might find it easy to carry on a conversation dressed only in a towel, Rachel thought, but she was having difficulty being so nonchalant about it. His bare upper body could have been sculptured by a master hand, and her fingers ached to stroke across his skin, feeling the corded muscles beneath it.

She dragged her mind back to the question he'd asked. "I told you before. I've been trying to sell this house. It seems like a waste of time and money to furnish this place, then turn around and sell everything when I move."

He settled his gaze on her. "Where will you go after you sell the house?"

Leaning her head back, she started to rock the chair with her foot. "I don't know. Maybe I'll go back to New York. Maybe I'll try Florida. I've also considered going to California. Since I can do my strip anywhere, I'm not limited to any one place."

His eyes narrowed as he picked out one of the comments she had made. "When did you live in New York?"

"Before I moved here," she answered briefly. "Since there hasn't been anyone interested in this house, it doesn't look as if I'll have to make a decision about where I'm going anytime soon."

He sipped his coffee as he thought about what she had said. She rarely let any information slip about herself. He had to grab each tidbit and store it up like a miser with pieces of gold. She had just explained a great deal. Ever since he had met her, he'd doubted her sense of style and sophistication had been honed in a small town like Bowersville. He had been right. What she had been doing in New York was still a question he wanted answered.

"New York, Florida, California," he said. "It sounds like Fannie isn't the only Gypsy."

She stopped rocking. "I'm not a Gypsy."

"Fannie doesn't have a desire to stay in any one place for long, and you apparently don't either. What would you call that if not a Gypsy?"

Getting out of her chair, she walked over to the tray and set her cup down. "I haven't found any one place where I feel I belong. When I find it, I'll stay there. Until then, I guess I keep looking."

"Maybe it's not a place but a person," he said quietly. "Have you ever considered that?"

She met his thoughtful gaze for a long moment. Then she slowly shook her head. "No. I never thought of that." And she didn't want to think of it now. Gesturing toward the coffeepot, she said, "Help yourself to the coffee. I'm going to check on your clothes."

Thorn stayed where he was. He had been given a few more pieces of the puzzle, but there were still more to fit into place. His gaze shifted back to the window while he went over everything Rachel had told him.

While she was gone, the phone beside her bed rang. Evidently she answered it downstairs, as it didn't ring again. Then he heard her call his name.

Going to the door, he saw her hurrying up the stairs, his clothing in her arms. "What's up?"

"Because of the heavy rain, the river is rising." She tossed him his clothing. "That was the mayor's wife on the phone. They need help sandbagging the river around the bridge to try to prevent the main road from flooding."

She brushed past him and yanked a pair of jeans off the shelf on her closet. As he shrugged into his shirt, he watched her open a dresser drawer and take out a cotton sweater. "What are you doing?"

"Changing clothes. I'm not exactly dressed for shoveling sand."

"You're going to go to the river?"

With her clothing clutched in her arms, she said, "Of course. If the river floods the bridge, it could make the road out of town impassable for quite a while. A load of sand from the quarry has just been dumped near the grain elevator. Some of the townspeople have started sandbagging, but they need more help."

He surprised her by chuckling. "And you don't think you belong here?"

Twenty minutes later they arrived at the river. Rachel had grabbed a raincoat on her way out of the house, but Thorn's clothes were soon just as wet as they had been earlier. At least the temperature was relatively mild. He helped men and some teenage boys stack sandbags in place while Rachel assisted other women filling up more burlap bags with sand. They worked by the light from headlights and spotlights of cars and trucks pointed toward the river.

Everyone felt a sense of urgency as the rain continued to fall in a steady downpour. Over the years, erosion had lowered the banks of the river on either side of the bridge. If the river flooded, there was a good chance the bridge would be washed out. If that happened, the town would be virtually stranded.

The sandbags became heavier as the night wore on and exhaustion set in. Mud coated boots and pant legs, and made each step precarious. Men slipped and fell. Muscles ached. The rain pelted down from the dark sky. No one quit. They took breaks for hot coffee and to rest, but not one person left, no matter how tired or uncomfortable he or she was.

At one point it looked as if Mother Nature was going to win the battle. The river began lapping at the top of the line of bags, and everyone worked faster.

Mr. Grundy was a tough taskmaster. He paced back and forth across the bridge, checking the temporary barriers on each side of the river. He was experienced in the ways of the river during a flood and was the self-appointed foreman.

When one of the men lost his footing and slipped into the river, it was Mr. Grundy who grabbed his hand and pulled him out of the strong current. When another man got a nasty splinter in his hand from the wooden supports of the bridge, it was Mr. Grundy who brought him over to Thorn to have it removed. After tugging out the sliver of wood and wrapping the man's hand in Mr. Grundy's handkerchief, Thorn wasn't surprised that the man went right back to stacking sandbags.

Working over by the grain elevator, Rachel felt the strain between her shoulder blades as she lifted another shovelful of sand. Mrs. Samuelson held the burlap bag open so Rachel could fill it. A half hour earlier Rachel had thought her duties as sand shoveler had come to an end when the pile of sand was nearly gone. Then a truck had pulled up with another large load and dumped it out on the pavement.

One of the women who had worked alongside Rachel most of the night had stated, "This is exactly like housework. Just when you think you're done, it piles up again."

Chuckling, the women continued filling bags with the sand. Rachel was a bit disconcerted to see a woman who was twenty years older than she working nonstop. She was almost dead on her feet. She paused for a minute and rested on her shovel, gazing over toward the river. It took her a moment to find Thorn's tall frame among the other men. Someone had lent him a black poncho, but she still recognized him. He was working steadily with the other men, as muddy and wet as everyone else.

While she watched, she saw his head turn as several of the men pointed downstream. She heard them shouting but couldn't make out what they said.

Beside her, Mae Kruger said, "Something's happened."

Rachel dropped her shovel and followed Mae up the side of the huge mound of sand in order to get a better view. They couldn't see anything until one of the spotlights was aimed on the churning water. A tree had torn loose from the bank farther upriver. The strong current carried it along, making it a floating missile as it aimed toward one of the supports of the bridge.

The men stood helpless on the bank of the river. Mr. Grundy watched from his vantage point on the bridge, disregarding the shouted warnings that the bridge might collapse.

All work was suspended as everyone watched the tree, its roots extended like gnarled fingers reaching out to grab anything in its path. It seemed to take forever for it to reach the bridge, even though the current was dangerously swift.

They all held their breaths as the tree bumped one of the bridge supports with a thud. Then the current nudged it toward the center of the river, and it passed under the bridge without doing any damage.

It took a few seconds for everyone to realize the danger was over, at least for the moment. Then they all laughed or exclaimed about the close call and resumed their work.

An hour later, when it looked as if they might be ahead of the rising water, Thorn took a break. He joined some of the others gathered around the back of Mr. Piggot's station wagon where Eliza Piggot had set up a large coffee urn. After accepting a steaming cup of coffee, he moved aside and saw Rachel leaning wearily against the front fender of the wagon.

Her jeans from her knees down were covered in mud and sand, and there was a streak of rich black dirt across her cheek. Several strands of her hair were plastered to the side of her face by the rain running off the hood of her raincoat. She appeared oblivious of the condition of her clothing or any discomfort due to the pouring rain.

Off and on during the last few hours he had looked over where she was filling burlap bags with sand. Once she laughed at something one of the other women said, her face turned upward while the rain sluiced over her cheeks and into her mouth. He couldn't imagine any other woman of his acquaintance doing what she was doing without complaint. Or one who affected him as strongly as she did. No matter how she was dressed or whatever circumstances he found her in, she attracted him like a moth to a flame.

She didn't have a cup of coffee, so he shared his. "Here. Take a taste of this and give me your opinion. Is this really coffee?"

Wrapping her hands around his, she took a sip. Considering she usually took great pains not to be touched by him, the casual gesture floored Thorn. Because it was so rare, it meant more than it would have otherwise.

She made a face and released the cup. "I think some of the mud from the Little Sioux River made it into this coffee."

Overcome by the need to feel her smiling lips under his, to find a release for the emotions welling up inside him, he lowered his head. But he stopped when he realized they weren't alone. Looking down into her face, he saw her eyes darken and her smile fade, and knew she had been aware of his intentions.

A voice from behind him called his name, breaking the intimate spell weaving around them.

Turning, Thorn saw Mr. Grundy coming toward them. Despite the oversize rubber boots on his feet, he strode quickly over the muddy ground, denying the elements of nature and his age. His black-hooded raincoat flapped around his legs. Stopping in front of Thorn, he nodded a brief greeting to Rachel, then came right to the point.

"How are you at delivering babies, Doc?"

"Rusty," he replied bluntly. "Is this a rhetorical question or do you have a particular reason for asking?"

"Marne Faber's neighbor just drove in and said Marne's in a bad way. He wanted to take her to the hospital in Algona, but she wouldn't go. Said she was waiting for her husband to come home. Trouble is, it don't look like the baby's going to wait."

"Where's her husband?"

"He's a truck driver and isn't due home for another couple of days. What about it, Doc? Think you can help her out?"

Thorn looked up at the unrelenting rain. "I'd need a four-wheel drive and directions."

Mr. Grundy nodded. "Rachel knows the Faber farm. She can show you how to get there." If he heard Rachel's quick intake of breath, he didn't give her an opportunity to protest. "Sam Pierce will lend you his Bronco. Some of the women offered to go, but this being Mrs. Faber's first and all, it'd be best to have a doctor on hand. We was hoping you would go."

Thorn glanced at Rachel and grinned. "Do you feel like a drive in the country?"

What she knew about delivering babies could be put in a thimble, she thought. But in a way it was her fault the townspeople knew Thorn would help in emergencies. "I don't know how much assistance I can give, but I can boil water."

She ended up doing a great deal more than boiling the water. If there had been time to think about what she was agreeing to do, she might have changed her mind. As it turned out, she wouldn't have missed the experience for anything in the world.

They took the time to stop at Edith's house so Thorn could swiftly shower, put on clean clothes, and to pick up his medical bag. Then while Thorn waited in the truck, Rachel ran into her house to exchange her muddy jeans for a dry pair. Once they passed the town limits of Bowersville, Rachel gave Thorn directions to the Faber farm. The gravel roads were rutted and full of water-filled potholes, but they were in better condition than the muddy lane leading to the Faber farmhouse.

Jerking the wheel to avoid a particularly treacherous dip in the road, Thorn commented, "It doesn't look like this guy Faber stays home much."

"He needs the extra income from trucking to supplement the income from the farm. I came out here with your aunt last spring when Marne had a sale of quilts and crafts she had made during the winter. Both Marne and her husband want to lease more land next year, and with the baby coming, they need all the money they can get."

Thorn had to maneuver the truck around ridges and deep ruts before finally reaching the house. It seemed as though every light was on in it. He parked as close to the house as he could, but they still had about forty feet to cover in the rain.

As soon as they were inside, the sounds of a woman in distress had Thorn taking the stairs two at a time. By the time Rachel reached the upstairs bedroom, Thorn was sitting on the side of the bed talking to Marne in a low voice, holding her hand.

From the doorway Rachel smiled at Marne. "I guess I don't have to make introductions."

"We haven't gotten as far as names yet," Marne said in a strained voice.

Introductions were the last thing on Marne's mind when she suddenly clenched Thorn's hand as she had a contraction. After that Marne didn't appear to care who Thorn was. She had other priorities that claimed her attention about every three minutes, then every two minutes. Thorn talked to her in a calm, persuasive voice, his quiet confidence easing her fears about what was happening to her. It eased Rachel's fears too.

Unless Thorn wanted her to fetch something, Rachel sat beside the bed holding Marne's hand and wiping the woman's face with a cool cloth. With each contraction Marne's fingers would tighten painfully around Rachel. As the night dragged on, Rachel was in awe of the woman's courage as she endured each contraction without uttering a sound.

Rachel had always thought she would have a baby sometime in the future. Now she wasn't so sure she wanted to go through the grinding agony she saw in Marne's eyes and felt every time Marne clutched her hand.

As early dawn began to lighten the sky, Thorn told

Marne to start pushing. Then he quietly called Rachel's name. She looked up, and he made a slight gesture with his head, indicating he wanted her. She untangled her fingers from Marne's grasp and joined him at the foot of the bed.

"I'm going to need your help," he said in a soft voice.

Shoving aside a feeling of panic, she asked, "What can I do?"

"Once the baby comes out, I'll need you to hold it. There's a bottle of alcohol on the table. Pour it over your hands. There isn't time for you to scrub up."

Rachel wanted to refuse, but she knew he wouldn't have asked for her help unless there was a good reason. With her heart in her throat she did as she was told.

He bent down and told Marne to push one last time. The baby dropped into his hands, and he gestured for Rachel to hold it. As he quickly tied the cord, she saw where it was loosely knotted just above the baby's navel. Suddenly she realized the danger the child had been in.

Thorn rubbed the baby vigorously with a towel, and the infant began to wail. Grinning broadly, he announced to Marne she had a healthy baby boy.

Rachel thought she would always remember the expression on Thorn's face when he held up the kicking infant to show Marne her son. His eyes radiated the supreme satisfaction of helping to bring a living human being into the world. She turned to look at Marne and saw the reflected joy in the woman's eyes at the sight of her baby, at the sound of his strong cry.

When Thorn handed Rachel the baby wrapped in

a blanket, her first reaction was fear she would drop the little bundle. Then as she looked down at the infant, she felt something move deep inside her and clutch her heart. She lifted her free hand and gently touched the baby's cheek with the back of her fingers. He was so tiny, so defenseless, yet so solid and alive.

Enraptured by the baby, she wasn't aware of Thorn watching her . . . or of the incredibly gentle smile he saw on her lips as she gazed down at the infant.

Walking over to the bed, she placed the living bundle in Marne's arms. As she gazed down at the mother and her son, Rachel felt envy. Marne had someone who was part of her, someone who belonged to her. Looking up, she found Thorn's attention was also on Marne and her baby. Then he raised his gaze, and his eyes locked with hers. He smiled as though he understood what she was feeling, because he felt it too.

Even though Marne and Thorn had done all the work, by the time the new mother and her baby had fallen asleep, Rachel was exhausted. She sank down in a rocking chair and leaned her head against its hard back. Thorn had left the room with the instruments he had used, taking them to the kitchen to clean them.

She was asleep in two minutes.

When Thorn returned to the bedroom, he stopped beside the chair and smiled down at Rachel. Then he lifted her in his arms and carried her out of the room. Leaving the door open so he could hear Marne or the baby, he took Rachel into another bedroom and gently lowered her to the bed.

He removed her shoes and covered her with a quilt. He might be exhausted, but he wasn't dead.

He didn't trust himself to take off any of her clothing. Kicking off his own shoes, he stretched out beside her, weariness flowing through every muscle in his body.

When Rachel rolled onto her side and faced him, he thought she was still asleep until she spoke. "What you did tonight was wonderful."

"I can't take any of the credit. Marne and Mother Nature did all the work."

She disagreed. "I watched you. She was very frightened when we first arrived. You talked her through the whole thing in a way that gave her confidence and made it easier for her." She paused, then asked, "What would have happened if you hadn't been here? I saw the cord was tied in a knot. That could mean there was a chance the baby could have died, doesn't it?"

"I felt it when I examined her. It was a loose knot, but it could have tightened during the birth process. I didn't want to take that chance, and that's why I wanted you to take the baby."

"It must be a wonderful feeling to be able to bring another life into the world."

He had been so preoccupied during the last few hours, he hadn't had time to think about what he was doing. His training had taken over, and he had done what he needed to do. Now he recalled the satisfaction he had felt when he held that newborn life in his hands. It was more than he had ever gotten from treating broken bones or operating on damaged knees.

Rachel yawned. "I can't remember ever feeling so tired and so exhilarated all at the same time."

He slipped his arm under her to bring her against

his side. "Try to get some sleep. You've had a busy day and night."

It didn't occur to her to resist. She rested her cheek against his chest and mumbled sleepily. "Aren't we going back to town?"

He closed his eyes out of weariness and to absorb the feel of her resting against him. He stroked her hair lightly, soothing both of them. "Not yet. We'll get a couple of hours sleep first. The rain has stopped but the roads will still be in pretty bad shape. I wouldn't want to drive us into a ditch because I was too tired to stay on the road."

"Will Marne and the baby be all right on their own after we're gone?"

"Some of the women in town will take turns coming out to stay with her until her husband gets home. I phoned Mr. Grundy while I was downstairs. He told me to call him no matter what time it was, so I did. He had just gotten back to his house. The sandbags are holding, and the rain is letting up. Several men are staying at the bridge to keep an eye on the situation, but everyone else has gone home. He also told me that Marne's neighbors take care of the stock when her husband's gone, so we don't have to worry about that."

"That's good," she muttered. "I don't know how to milk a cow."

Her cheek nuzzled his shoulder as she tried to find a more comfortable position. She made a murmuring sound which could have meant anything. A few seconds later he felt her body slacken and heard her breathing deepen. Pulling half of the quilt over himself, he closed his eyes.

A strange feeling of peace settled on him as he

adjusted Rachel's weight until she was partially lying on top of him. He couldn't believe three days earlier he had actually thought Bowersville was a dull town. Every day he had been in the small town had provided new experiences and surprises, none more important than meeting Rachel Hyatt.

Her presence, her touch, her nearness, gave his life a certain grace, a strength and a pleasure he had never known and didn't want to live without.

His arms tightened around her. He couldn't think of another thing he needed at the moment. All aspects of his life as a doctor and as a man had come together. His clever aunt had known what he needed all along, even when he didn't, and had been instrumental in pushing him into finding it.

He fell into the oblivion of sleep with the scent of Rachel in his nostrils and the warmth of her in his blood.

Seven

Rachel woke gradually. It wasn't a matter of simply opening her eyes, but of crawling out of a deep fog. Awareness crept over her slowly.

Since she had never slept with anyone before, the slight weight across her legs and under her breasts shocked her fully awake. Turning slightly she saw Thorn's head beside hers on the pillow.

Lying completely still so she wouldn't waken him, she allowed herself the freedom of studying him while he slept. She needed to soak up the sight of him against the time when he would be gone. During the last couple of days he had turned her upside down and inside out. He had stirred her up and knocked down her defenses with the ease of a whirlwind blowing through a house of straw.

It was odd that she wasn't more upset about the upheaval he had caused in her life. It was one of the things she was going to have to think about when she was alone.

Daylight filtered through the window on the other side of the small bedroom. She had no conception of time, and at the moment she didn't particularly care if it was morning or afternoon. She absorbed the strength and warmth of Thorn along her side. The intimacy of his arm pressed against the underside of her breasts felt oddly natural and right. It was as though she was where she belonged because she was with Thorn.

Suddenly she closed her eyes against the onslaught of emotions storming through her. She loved him. That was the only explanation she could come up with to describe the feelings he created within her. It was probably the dumbest thing she had ever done, yet it was impossible to deny. Just because it was an emotion she had never experienced before didn't lessen its intensity. Whether he wanted her love or not, it was hers to give. And she had given it to him.

She opened her eyes, and her gaze collided with his.

His voice was husky with sleep, his smile warmly intimate. "Good morning."

"Good morning." Her reply was quiet and restrained.

"I should go check on our patient, but I'm too comfortable where I am."

More for something to say than wanting to know, she said, "I wonder what time it is."

"I don't know. You're lying on my watch." When she started to move away so he could free his arm, his fingers spread across her rib cage. "No. Stay where you are. I don't care what time it is."

"We have to get up."

The scent of her hair, her sweet womanly fragrance, tightened his hold and his body. "Why?"

"We can't stay in bed all day," she murmured, trying to be practical.

Moving closer, he nuzzled her neck. "Why not?"

His warm breath against her skin made her tremble. "Marne and the baby might need us."

Lifting his head, he looked down into her eyes, seeing the shimmering desire in their depths. He slid his hand over her waist to her hip and pressed her lower body into his. "I'm beginning to have a few needs of my own."

"Thorn," she said, alarmed to hear the yearning in her voice when she had meant to warn him off. "Nothing's changed."

He brushed his mouth over her mouth, his tongue dragging across her bottom lip. "That's true. I want you just as much as I did when I saw you in the river."

Her body betrayed her by yielding to the pressure of his hand caressing her hip. "I meant I'm still inexperienced. You don't want that. Last night . . ."

"Last night you misunderstood why I pulled away from you." Propping himself up on an elbow, he gazed down at her, his expression serious and compelling. "Your first time should be with tenderness, the loving gentle and caring. I wanted you too badly to be any of those things, so I backed off. You deserve more than I could have given you then."

Afraid he would see too much in her eyes, she lowered her lashes, but he wouldn't let her hide from him. He brought his hand up to touch her jaw. When she raised her eyes to his, he went on. "I know you have your reasons for not wanting to commit yourself to me. Whatever they are, we'll over-come them and be together the way we should be."

He lowered his head, his mouth grazing hers. "In the meantime . . ."

She shuddered. Her heart thudded as he parted her lips and took her to the depths of sensuality he had introduced into her life. Unable to fight off the aggressive demand to respond, she twined her arms around his neck, her hips pressing into his.

Smoldering embers of need burst into flames as Thorn deepened his assault on her mouth. When he had kissed her before, her tentative responses had tantalized and challenged him. Having her meet his passion equally was devastating.

He drew his hand over her hip, down her thigh, and back to her hip. When he felt her hand follow the same pattern down his side, he ground his aroused body into hers. Not trusting himself to with-stand the feel of her naked flesh, he ran his fingers over her breast with her shirt as a barrier. The soft material became part of the caress, evoking visions of silken skin and womanly curves.

His heartbeat throbbed loudly in his ears, almost drowning out the husky moan she made when she pressed her breast into his hand. In a small, still-sane section of his mind, he marveled at the explo-sive passion coursing through him just by touching her clothed body. Naked, she would tear apart his control and shatter his need to be gentle.

"Thorn," she groaned against his neck. "I'm not like this."

"Yes, you are." His hand left her breast and skimmed over her ribs and hips to press against the apex of her thighs. He was rewarded with a thrusting of her lower body into his hand and a soft, tortured sigh. "This is the real Rachel," he murmured hoarsely as he looked deep into her passion-glazed eyes.

She threaded her fingers through his hair, forcing his head down. Her needs overcame her inhibitions, and she made aggressive demands of her own.

It was the first time she had instigated a kiss, and Thorn's mind reeled with the knowledge.

Suddenly a foreign sound ripped apart the sensual cloud that enveloped them. Realizing what it was, Thorn buried his face in her neck for a moment, absorbing the moist scent of her flesh.

He reluctantly raised his head, his gaze locking with hers. "The baby."

Realization came slowly into her eyes. A soft tinge of color spread over her cheeks as she recalled her abandoned response to his lovemaking.

"You make the world disappear," she said softly.

Stunned by her admission, he stared down at her. She was making it damn difficult to be sensible. The demanding cry from the baby penetrated the walls of the bedroom, a warning that their time alone had come to an end.

Levering himself off her, he stood beside the bed and held out his hand. "Let's take care of the baby."

Rachel didn't take his hand immediately. Holding his gaze with her own, she knew they had crossed an invisible line. What happened next was a mystery, but she realized it was one she was willing to solve.

Lifting her hand, she clasped his and felt his fingers closing around hers.

• • •

While they were attending to Marne and the baby's needs, a woman from town arrived with a hamper full of food. Mrs. Pearsall was a motherly woman who had grandchildren of her own. Unfortunately they lived in another state, and she saw them rarely. The opportunity to help a new mother cope with a baby was a joy, not a chore.

Thorn and Rachel left the farmhouse after eating the lunch Mrs. Pearsall had pressed on them. During the drive back to town, they kept the topic of conversation centered on Marne and the baby.

When Thorn turned onto the highway, leaving the last rutted graveled road behind, he glanced at Rachel. "It just occurred to me I haven't thanked you for helping me last night. I couldn't have done it without you."

She choked back a laugh. "Of course you could. All I did was fetch and carry and follow your instructions."

"I was glad you were there. I needed all the moral support I could get."

She stared at him. "Why? You're a terrific doctor."

Her compliment pleased him more than it would have coming from anyone else. "I haven't delivered a baby since I was an intern. I admit to having a few moments of panic, especially when I realized the cord was knotted."

"I don't believe you. You knew exactly what you were doing every minute."

He smiled. "It was more a case of nature taking its inevitable course without any help from me." He slowed the car as they entered the town limits. "I don't know about you, but I need a shower and some clean clothes."

"I feel a little grungy myself."

"Do you want me to drop you off at your place?" Suddenly he hit the steering wheel with the palm of his hand. "Damn!"

Startled, Rachel asked, "What's the matter?"

"I didn't even think about your work. Has helping me put you behind on your comic strip?"

She shrugged. "Don't worry about it."

He glanced at her. "That's it? Don't worry about it? You're going to have to do better than that, Rachel. You have as many rights in this relationship as I do. We don't automatically do everything my way." His gaze flicked to her again. "If we did, I would take you home with me and not let you out of my bed for a week. I want you to tell me if you need to work."

His words caused tantalizing pictures to form in her mind of tangled sheets and moist, hot skin rubbing against hers. Clearing her throat, she admitted, "I should work."

He took her at her word, turning in the direction of her house rather than his aunt's. "All right."

Rachel remained silent as he pulled into her driveway. She didn't know the procedure, the rules for behavior after spending the night with a man. They hadn't made love, but there had been an intimacy of a different kind, changing the relationship. To what she didn't know.

He left the engine running. Shifting to face her, he asked, "What time do you think you'll be through?"

"Around four o'clock."

He reached across her and opened the door for her. "Should I pick you up about six, then?" Straightening up, he smiled as she nodded. "How about picnic down by the river? There's still all that food we have to get through."

"Do you have anything against eating indoors?" she asked with amusement. "Last night we ate under the willow tree and now you want to have a picnic by the river."

"Your house doesn't have any furniture in the dining room. If we stay at my aunt's where there are table and chairs, Mr. Grundy could show up wanting to play canasta, or someone could appear on the doorstep wanting a splinter taken out of their behind. At least sitting on a blanket on the bank of the river will be more pleasant than sitting on the floor in your dining room."

The only thing that mattered to Rachel was that she would be with him. "I'll see you at six, then. Unless something else comes up. So far we've had a fire and a flood. They say things happen in threes. It's hard telling what will happen next."

The prospect of another disaster didn't seem to bother him much. "If the sun doesn't dry out the ground, we'll probably end up sliding into the river, food and all."

"I'll agree to go on a picnic on one condition."

"What's that?"

"Leave Edith's dandelion wine at home."

"You got it."

When Thorn returned, he didn't know if the woman he had come for was Rachel or Fancy Fannie. The clothing she had chosen was straight out of a Gypsy caravan. Her red skirt was full with a ruffle around the hem and an elaborate embroidery design on the bottom half. A white Cluny lace petticoat hung down several inches below the skirt. A wide cloth belt was wrapped around her waist, the two ends hanging down one side of her skirt.

It was what she wore on top that had made his mouth go dry the instant she opened the door.

The white camisole hugged her upper body, ending at the top curve of her breasts with narrow straps over her slender shoulders. There were no buttons or zippers but laces criss-crossing up the front, ending in a loose bow between her breasts.

Dressed in a black shirt and gray slacks, he felt like a drab crow beside a beautiful peacock.

Once they were at the river, Thorn found a secluded spot to spread out a blanket. Rachel had been unusually quiet during the drive and still didn't say much after the food had been set out on the blanket.

In place of the dandelion wine, Thorn had brought lemonade. He poured her a glass and handed it to her. "Rachel, what's wrong? You haven't said two words since we left your house."

"I received a phone call this afternoon from the realtor in Algona. She had a client who might be interested in several pieces of property I've been trying to sell."

"That's great news." He saw her face. "Isn't it?"

"The property they're interested in are two lots on the main street. The lots are occupied. Peabody's and Ruby's Café."

Sitting back on his heels, he was puzzled why she wasn't happier at the prospect of selling some of her property. "I thought the reason you came back to

Bowersville was to sell your grandfather's land. This is a start."

"You don't understand. The realtor said the client wouldn't be interested in leasing the property to the existing tenants as my grandfather did, and as I still do. The client needs a tax writeoff, which means he wants a negative cash flow. The buildings would be torn down."

Thorn didn't respond right away. Finally he uttered, "Oh."

"Yes. Oh. I can't do that to the people whose lives depend on the income they earn in their businesses. I'd be responsible for destroying Mrs. Lindstrom's way of life and affecting a great many others' by selling a grocery store out from under the whole town. How can I jeopardize a person's livelihood just because I want to sell some property?"

"Apparently you can't. Since this is the only offer you've gotten in over a year, it looks like you're going to have to either hold out for another buyer or accept the fact you aren't going to sell it. There are worse places to live. You might find you want to stay if you bought some furniture and made that house livable."

She reached over and took a pickle off his plate. "And what will you do about Edith's house?"

"I'm keeping it."

She almost choked on the bite of pickle she had taken. "It's a helluva commute between Bowersville and Des Moines."

"True," he said agreeably.

He didn't want to talk about houses and land. He was more interested in thinking about the results if he pulled one of the lacing ends dangling between her breasts. He had a pretty good idea what would happen . . . and it was driving him crazy.

"What would you do with the house, then?" she asked. "Just leave it empty?"

He shook his head. Bringing his gaze back to her face, he said, "It isn't that far to drive for a weekend."

She wanted to believe he would spend his weekends in Bowersville in order to see her, but she didn't want to look like a fool by asking him in case that wasn't what he meant.

Because she didn't want him to know how important it was to her what he did on his weekends, she continued talking about her property. "Something the realtor said gave me an idea what to do about my business properties."

Thorn was disappointed. He had hoped she would be interested enough to follow up on his comment about his weekends. Striving for patience, he asked, "What idea was that?"

"That the rent the tenants are paying now could be applied toward the purchase of the property. I could make the same arrangements with the people living in the houses. The only house I wouldn't be able to dispose of would be my grandfather's. What do you think?"

"I'd say it was up to you."

Rachel watched, puzzlement creasing her brow as he suddenly sprang off the blanket. He walked over to a tree growing near the edge of the river. Leaning a shoulder against the sturdy trunk, he watched the slowly rolling water.

"Thorn?"

He turned but stayed where he was. "You don't get it, do you? I'm talking about planning on how I can spend more time in Bowersville, and you're trying to figure out how in hell you can get away. Excuse me if I don't help you do it."

Her skirt got tangled in her legs as she struggled to her feet. Facing him, she said, "I haven't asked you for your help, have I?"

"No. That's part of the problem. You don't ask me for anything." Planting his hands on his hips, he demanded, "Tell me one thing. Is it Bowersville you're so eager to get away from, or is it me?"

Was it her imagination, or was he hurt as well as angry, she wondered as she searched his eyes. "I've been trying to sell my grandfather's property since long before I met you, Thorn. The one hasn't anything to do with the other."

He studied her, frustration stiffening his back and shoulders. After a long, tense moment, he shook his head. "It's not going to work, is it?"

Bewildered she stared at him. "What isn't going to work?"

"Us." Thorn saw her flinch. If he had slapped her, he didn't think she would look any more shocked than she did at that moment. He steeled himself against her hurt expression. "Evidently I've been wrong in assuming there was even an us. You don't tell me anything unless I use a crowbar to get it out of you. The only time you've shown me I have anything you might want is when I kiss you. Otherwise you don't need me. I know I'm stubborn, even pigheaded when I want something, but I'd like to think I stop short of making a fool of myself."

He came back to the blanket and knelt down. With quick efficient movement he gathered their plates, glasses, and the containers of food, and stacked them back into the hamper.

Rachel stood several feet away and watched him pack up their picnic without offering to help. She felt numb and unable to respond or accomplish the simplest task.

The ride back to her house was carried out in silence, an uncomfortable silence. Thorn had said enough, and Rachel hadn't said a thing.

When he parked behind her car in her driveway, he left the motor running. With both hands clenching the wheel, he stared straight ahead.

Rachel knew he was waiting for her to get out of his car, but she didn't move. She realized she was at a crossroad. She could take the safe road with a smooth surface free of potholes and ruts. And be alone. Or she could take the other road, which was anything but safe and would have more than its share of bumps and detours. And possibly be with Thorn.

With her heart in her throat she abruptly leaned over and turned the key in the ignition before she changed her mind. Then she pulled the key out, opened her door, and stepped from the car. The irregular ridges of the various keys on his key ring dug into her palm as she clenched her hand and started for her front door.

As she placed her hand on the door latch, she heard the slam of a car door. The sound was almost as loud as the thudding of her heart.

Stepping inside, she stopped at the foot of the stairs. She had gone as far as she could go in more ways than one. Her only thought had been to keep him from leaving, but now she had to find the words to make him stay. Whenever she had wanted something, she had had to fight to get it and to keep it. Her relationship with Thorn, if they were to have one, depended on her saying the right things. She was going to have to overcome her natural reticence and expose her feelings, or she was going to lose him.

She turned slowly when she heard his footsteps on the wooden porch. Still clutching his keys she lifted her chin and faced him.

He stood just inside the door. "Can I have my car keys?"

"No."

He took a deep, weary breath. "Why prolong this, Rachel? Just give me my keys and I'll be on my way."

Her fingers tightened painfully around the keys. "You're wrong."

"About what?"

His abrupt tone wasn't encouraging. Since her knees were a trifle unsteady, she sank down onto one of the steps and clasped her hands together on her knees, his keys held between her palms. She swallowed with difficulty, then managed to say, "I do have needs, but it's hard for me to talk about them."

"Why?"

He wasn't going to make it easy for her. She was holding her hands so tightly, her knuckles were turning white. "I'm not comfortable talking about my feelings."

"Why?"

"Basically because I haven't had much practice. My grandfather barely said three words in a day and wasn't much better about listening. One day I rebelled against his rule about pets by bringing home a kitten. He made me give it back to the woman who was giving the kittens away. Two days later I was shipped off to a boarding school in a suburb of New York. At the time I didn't realize he had made the plans long before the kitten incident. I remember being afraid I would be sent to an orphanage or a convent if I made him mad again."

She looked up at Thorn. His expression was unreadable, but at least he was listening.

"After that, the few times I tried to stand up to him I ended up losing my dinner." She gave him a self-deprecating smile. "It's difficult to make a point effectively when you're throwing up. Over the years I've learned there are different ways of handling people and situations other than by direct confrontation."

He left the door and sat down on the step beside her. Leaning back, he rested his forearms on the stair behind him. "Why are you telling me this now? Why not earlier?"

Fixing her gaze on her clasped hands she murmured, "Some risks are necessary to take. I wanted you to understand why it's hard for me to open up to anyone, even to you."

Her last three words indicated he was special to her and wiped away the lingering threads of anger. He sat forward and placed his hand under her chin to force her to look at him. "I'm not asking you to give up anything, Rachel, nor do I want you to go anywhere or be anybody but yourself. I just need to know who you are, how you feel about things, about me, about us. I want a personal intimate relationship with you, which means we have to start communicating on more than a physical level."

Lifting her hand, she wrapped her fingers around his wrist. "Since we don't have as many difficulties communicating physically, perhaps that would be a good place to start."

Shock waves shook Thorn. She had met him half-way and even taken a few steps beyond. That she was willing to leap even further had him reeling. Stroking her bottom lip with his thumb, he asked quietly, "Are you sure that's what you want?"

"Don't make me go into my reasons, Thorn. I'm about all talked out."

He smiled for the first time since they had left the river. "You're right. Some things don't have to be discussed."

His lips replaced his thumb, his teeth nipping at her lips. He was in no hurry now. Even though his needs were as strong as ever, he wanted to savor every stroke of his tongue, each caress of her body.

Getting to his feet, he pulled her up with him. His keys clattered to the floor, but neither of them cared. Thorn lifted her easily in his arms and started up the stairs.

Eight

His gaze remained on her face as he lowered her to her feet beside her bed. Slowly he raised his hand to the laces between her breasts. He gently tugged on one end, and his attention drifted down her neck to the white material parting as the loose bow came untied. The soft bare mounds of her breasts were gradually exposed.

He raised his eyes to meet hers. She stood motionless, a trace of shyness in the dark depths of her eyes. But she didn't attempt to shield the flesh he had uncovered.

Lowering his head, he claimed her mouth. He didn't bother to conceal his hunger, but he kept it under control. Barely. As badly as he wanted to feel her body close around his, he wanted to prolong this first time. For himself as well as for her.

His hands slid under her top to her breasts. The air seemed to crackle around them with a sensual current, sensitizing their nerve endings. Rachel's eyes closed, and she threw her head back as pleasure flowed through her in waves. She brought her hands up to enclose his wrists, applying pressure.

"Am I supposed to ache like this?" she asked, opening her eyes to stare at him. "Is aching supposed to feel this good?"

Thorn found it difficult to speak. She was so breathtakingly beautiful with desire glazing her eyes, her body trembling under his hands. There weren't words in any language to describe how wonderful she looked and felt.

His mouth against her throat, he assured her, "It's never been like this before for me, Rachel. In a way, this will be a first time for me too."

His arms came around her waist, bringing her soft breasts against his chest, her hips into the waiting cradle of his. She gasped and breathed his name, her lower body arching against him as she instinctively sought relief from the torment of passion.

Unable to resist her uncontrolled response, Thorn lowered her onto the bed, following her down. He kissed her again and again, his control fading away with each brush of her tongue answering the wordless plea of his mouth.

As the sky darkened into night, their passion rose in a fever heat. Clothing was stripped away, needs growing and demanding release.

Needing to slow down the rush of passion, Thorn pushed back from her, allowing himself the luxury of simply looking at her. She gazed up at him, her lips moist from his kisses, her eyes softly sensual. He looked for fear or wariness and found neither. Her eyes were clear as she met his gaze.

Unable to keep from touching her, he stroked her

thigh. "You feel like warm satin." Then the curving slope of her hips. "Warm and incredibly soft." He finally stopped his caress at her breast. "And here you are woman, feminine and fascinating."

He saw her eyes change as his thumb rubbed over her nipple, could almost feel the heat of desire racing through her blood. Then she raised her hand toward him, and his heart thudded as her fingers threaded through the dark curling hairs on his chest.

"I never believed fairy tales could come true," she said, her voice soft and husky, flowing over him like warm whiskey on a cold night. "I never believed magic could be real. You've made me believe in both. You make me feel like Sleeping Beauty being awakened by a kiss from the prince."

"And the magic?" he asked, his own voice hoarse with barely suppressed need.

The tip of her finger copied the motion of his thumb stroking her nipple. "This is magic." She cupped the back of his neck, bringing his head down to her. Against his mouth, she whispered, "This is magic."

If he could have spoken, he would have disagreed with her. It wasn't magic, it was insanity to want a woman as badly as he did at that moment. Before he lost his mind completely, he raised his head to look down at her, needing to see her expression.

There was no fear, only desire glowing in the depths of her eyes. Her soft, womanly smile was an invitation, perhaps holding a trace of uncertainty, but definitely luring him toward her, not away.

"I have to have you, Rachel. I'm not sure I can hold back much longer. I want you too much."

"I want to belong to you, Thorn. If only for a little while."

Her legs twined around his as she ground her hips against his hard length, driving the last of his control away. His mouth claimed hers with an almost violent hunger, and he pulled her to him, crushing her breasts against his chest.

He felt her nails glide over his back, and gave in to her completely. Shuddering against her, he parted her legs with his knee and murmured her name against her throat. He accepted the invitation of her heated flesh, sinking into her as carefully as his desperate desire for her would allow. He thought he heard his name but couldn't be sure. Then it didn't matter.

A whirlpool of sensations pulled them down into the spiraling pleasure waiting for them in the depths of sensuality. Together they crashed upon the shore of completion, the waves of delight washing over them long after their passion had crested.

Time had no meaning as they lay together on Rachel's bed. Thorn couldn't find the strength to ease away from her, even though he knew he was too heavy for her slender frame. His heartbeat was anything but steady, his breathing only slowly returning to normal.

He had never felt more a man than he did at that moment. What had been sex with other women had been lovemaking with Rachel. That term had never been much more than a phrase before. Now it explained everything.

He was in love with her. He hadn't expected to fall in love with her. Want her, yes, but not love her. Hell, he had never thought he was even capable of feeling this intense need for another person. But love was the only explanation for the bond he felt with her. She was as necessary to him as the blood that flowed in his veins, the breath he took into his lungs.

Raising his head, he leaned on his forearms in order to see her face. He needed to see the woman who had become his life.

A light sheen of moisture dampened her skin. Her eyes were shut, her lips slightly parted. Discovering how he felt made it imperative he learn her feelings.

He murmured her name. She slowly raised her long lashes. Supreme satisfaction radiated from her dark eyes as she met his gaze.

"Are you all right?" he asked. "I didn't hurt you?"

A puzzled frown flickered across her face to be replaced by the sweetest, softest smile he had ever seen. Her hair slid over the pillow as she shook her head. "You made me feel wonderful." The frown returned. "Did I disappoint you?"

Her vulnerability created a tightness in his chest, as though he had taken on the burden of her insecurity. "How could I possibly be disappointed with finding the other half of myself? You were everything a man ever dreamed of. At least this man."

Her mouth went dry as she became aware of his body hardening inside her. She sighed softly, and he brushed his lips over hers, his hands skimming down her sides. The incredible sequence began again. This time their needs weren't as urgent but the passion was as strong and as immediate as before.

The rest of the week passed in a whirl of activity. Rachel stored up each moment with Thorn, her memory creating a mental scrapbook of every minute they spent together. The only thing they did that could be called exciting was their lovemaking. Everything else could be classed as normal. Trips to the grocery store, cooking meals, taking walks. However, Rachel couldn't consider any of those other activities normal since she had always done them alone before.

With Thorn she experienced a closeness she had never dreamed could exist between two people. The only point of friction between them was her insistence that they part for the night. She argued that it wouldn't take the neighbors long to realize she and Thorn were practically living together if his car was in her driveway in the early morning, or hers was parked in Edith's drive night after night. Rachel was too sensitive to the feelings of the community to offend their morality by openly flaunting her affair with Edith's nephew.

Thorn didn't like it. He understood, but he still hated it. Each time he left her house at the end of the evening, or she threw back the covers of his bed and left, he hated it more. He wanted the intimacy of holding her in the long dark hours of the night, to wake up with her beside him. Sneaking around as though their being together was something to be ashamed of became more frustrating as the days went by.

On Wednesday he accompanied her to each of the businesses her grandfather had left her so she could talk to the managers about applying their rent to the purchase of the property. After the initial shock they were willing to look over the contracts Rachel's lawyer had drawn up.

When they went to see Mrs. Lindstrom, who was still recovering from her back injury, she was resting on a couch in her cluttered living room. She had tears in her eyes at the thought of owning the business that had been in the family for three generations. Rachel's grandfather had refused to sell the café, and Mrs. Lindstrom had resigned herself to leasing the property. When Rachel asked her to look over the legal agreement, Mrs. Lindstrom signed the paper immediately, not needing any time to think it over.

In the car Thorn told Rachel she had just given the older woman the best medicine possible.

"It's funny," Rachel said thoughtfully. "Owning the café means so much to Mrs. Lindstrom, and I'm relieved to have one less property to worry about."

"Most people would be ecstatic to own half a town."

"I've never thought of any of the property as belonging to me. I still consider it all my grandfather's, not mine."

There was that word again, Thorn thought. She had used it before. "That means a lot to you, doesn't it? Belonging?"

During the last couple of days she had made an effort to talk more freely with Thorn, but her natural reticence made her pause. Being open about her feelings still wasn't easy, but she knew it was necessary to their relationship.

"There is a saying you don't miss what you never had. That's not altogether true."

"What is it you miss?"

"That's the odd part. I'm not sure. I've always felt something was missing in my life, as though I've never quite fit in somehow, never really belonged.

No matter where I've been, I've felt like an outsider." She laughed self-consciously. "Maybe everybody feels that way at some time or other."

"I remember the day I started medical school. As I went through the door to go to my first class, I wondered what in hell I was doing there. All the other men and women there seemed smarter, more qualified, and obviously dedicated. Everyone else appeared to be so confident as they sauntered down the hallway while I had a death grip on my books. Later, I learned everyone felt pretty much the way I did."

"You had a goal to work toward. It was your choice to become a doctor, so you attended medical school. Going to a girls' boarding school was not my idea."

"What was it like? I can't imagine going to a school where I didn't get to leave after classes were over."

"We lived in dormitories, wore uniforms, and went to class. Our dean didn't believe sports were appropriate for the health and well-being of properly brought up young ladies, so most of the time we stayed indoors. There were cliques of girls who chummed around together, according to their interests. The girls who were concerned about the latest fashions and hairdos clustered around magazines, living vicariously through them. The girls who were more interested in culture than haute couture spent their spare time practicing the piano or painting. The ones who preferred the sciences gathered to dissect some poor creature or figure out mathematical equations."

"Which group did you belong to?"

"A select group of one. I was more comfortable with my own company than trying to mix with strangers."

"My father once told me a stranger is just some-one you haven't met."

"My grandfather told me if you open a door, people expect to come in. It's better to keep the door closed."

Thorn felt hot anger rise in his blood. That old buzzard should never have been left in charge of a sensitive young girl. The hermit sent her away to live at a boarding school, then gave her the twisted gems of his so-called wisdom when she returned to Bowersville.

His wiser aunt had seen in Rachel what he had discovered. Underneath her cool exterior was a warm, passionate woman needing to love and be loved.

He reached over and enclosed her hand in his. "The door isn't ever going to be closed again. You belong with me. We belong together."

The warmth of his touch radiated up her arm into her heart. Her fingers tightened around his. She found it easy to believe they belonged together when she was with him. Maybe it was because she wanted to believe it so badly. Each touch, each smile, each word, each caress, reinforced what he said. There hadn't been any promises about the future, nor had he indicated they even had one. Every day was a gift she hadn't expected. She was going to take this interlude with him one day at a time, without insisting on guarantees of a lifetime.

On Thursday Rachel noticed Thorn appeared deep in thought at odd moments. She would catch him staring off into space, and once she had to repeat her statement about lunch being ready. That eve-ning they were at Edith's house, sorting through the various items Thorn's aunt had requested be sent to her in Hawaii. Thorn had gone into the kitchen to search for some tape to close the boxes with, and didn't come back for quite a while. Rachel went to find him. She was about to enter the kitchen when she heard him talking on the phone.

She heard him laugh and say, "I'm glad to hear Des Moines is surviving without me. How about my patients?" After a brief pause he continued. "I'll be at the clinic around nine tomorrow. I want to go to my apartment first. Tell Marty I'll need her all day. I might as well warn you now. I'm going to try to convince her she should come back with me." There was a moment of silence, then he chuckled. "It wouldn't be the first time I've stolen a woman from you."

Rachel retraced her steps to the living room but didn't continue wrapping the pieces of Edith's silver service. Instead, she sat down on the couch, crossing her arms as she went over Thorn's conversation. Her gaze settled on the black phone perched on a small table by one of the easy chairs. It didn't take a genius to figure out Thorn hadn't wanted her to overhear his phone call, or he would have used the living room phone. For someone who wanted everything up front between them, he was certainly acting secretive. In an attempt to rationalize, she reasoned that he might have thought of the need to call someone after he had entered the kitchen, but she discarded that notion as wishful thinking.

Not once in all the time they had been together had he implied he would be returning to Des Moines anytime soon. She wondered when he planned on telling her, or if he even was going to bother. She wished she knew what the last week had meant to him.

And who Marty was.

She bit her lip. What was she grousing about, she asked herself. In a short time he had changed her life. He had taught her a great deal about herself. One of the gifts he had given her was a sense of self-worth as a woman. His exclusive attention had made her feel desirable and feminine. She had discovered passionate depths within herself she had never suspected she had. She should be thankful instead of resentful.

She sighed heavily. While she was doing all this soul searching, she might as well admit she was also greedy. She wanted it all. And why shouldn't she have it, she wondered. Wasn't she the one who had fought to have her own comic strip against more odds than they offered in Las Vegas? She had won that fight. Maybe, just maybe, she could win this one as well. The trouble was she needed time to think of how to go about it, and time was one thing she was running out of since Thorn would be leaving tomorrow.

She got off the couch and walked over to the box she had been packing. As she wrapped the silver sugar bowl in a soft flannel cloth, she was surprised her hands weren't trembling. She felt like throwing something. She was furious with herself for not being experienced enough to come up with a way to hold on to Thorn.

Thorn sensed her anger the moment he came into the room. He didn't know the reason for it, but he was pleased to see it. Anger was better than indifference. She was a woman who needed stirring up, and he enjoyed doing the stirring. He had helped her remove some of the layers she had hidden her feelings under, but there were still more to uncover.

He handed her the packing tape. "Edith and her new husband had better have a big house if she's going to find room for all this stuff she wants. She's going to need a separate room just for the scrapbooks."

Rachel ripped the tape across the closed flaps of one of the boxes. Without commenting, she moved on to the next one and taped it too.

Piling one box on the other, he looked at her. "I'll mail these when I get back to Des Moines tomorrow."

She gave no sign she had heard him, or if she did, that she cared. "Did you hear what I said?" he asked. "I'm going to Des Moines in the morning."

She taped another box. "I heard you."

He wasn't getting the response he wanted. "Wouldn't you like to know why I'm leaving?"

"You have your practice in Des Moines. It's not too surprising you want to get back to it. You've stayed in Bowersville longer than I thought you would."

He was becoming irritated. She acted as if she couldn't care less. He took the roll of tape out of her hand and drew her over to the only chair that didn't have anything piled on top of it. "I think we'd better talk about this."

The phone rang, startling Rachel. She was closest to it but didn't answer. Thorn glanced at her sharply before reaching across her to pick it up.

"Dr. Cannon," he said automatically. He listened for a minute. "I'll be right there."

He slammed the phone down. "I have to run next door. Mr. Grundy isn't feeling well. I'll be back as soon as I can."

He hurried out of the room, picking up his medical bag on his way out the door. Rachel followed him to the porch, wondering if he was really going to leave in the middle of their conversation. Apparently he was, for he cut across the lawn, heading toward Mr. Grundy's house.

She had finished the packing and was sitting at Edith's antique desk writing him a note when he called.

"I'm going to stay with Mr. Grundy for a while," he said.

"Is he all right?"

He chuckled. "That is one tough old man."

"What happened?"

"Mr. Grundy thought he was having a heart attack. He refused to go to the hospital in Algona when I suggested he take some tests. Said he didn't like to go out at night. That if he was going to die, he'd rather do it at home. The pain in his chest turned out to be simple indigestion, a result of consuming two bowls of chili, a tunafish sandwich, and two cans of beer."

"But he's all right now?"

"He's feeling better. I fixed him a bicarbonate of soda. I'm going to stay with him for a while just to make sure he's okay." His amusement was evident in his voice. "He's in a talkative mood, telling me stories about his adventurous youth. If even half of them are true, Mr. Grundy has had an interesting life."

She crumpled up the paper she had written on. "I was going to leave you a note. All the packing is done. You won't be able to fit all of the boxes in your car, so leave the smaller ones here. I'll mail them to Edith the next time I go to Algona."

"Leave everything. I'll take care of it when I get back. I don't want you lifting any of the boxes." When she didn't reply, he wondered if she was still on the line. "Rachel?"

"I'm here."

In the background she could hear the sounds of guns going off and people shouting. "Lord," Thorn muttered, "Mr. Grundy's turned the volume of the TV up. I'll see you later. I shouldn't be too long, maybe another hour."

Rachel opened her mouth to speak, but the line went dead. She had been about to tell him she was going home and wouldn't be there when he returned. Hanging up the phone, she sat back down at the desk and wrote another note.

Two hours later she was propped up in bed reading when her phone rang. She put a bookmark at her place and picked up the phone.

Thorn's voice was heavy with fatigue and rough with temper. "I got your note. What in hell are you doing over there when you should be here?"

"It's late."

"I know what time it is, Rachel. I've been telling time for quite a while now. What I don't know is why you didn't wait for me here. We need to talk." He didn't wait for her to answer. "Hell, this is ridiculous. I'm tired of all this sneaking around. When I get back, there are going to be some major changes, so be prepared."

It was five days before Thorn had accomplished everything he had set out to do in Des Moines. Closing down his medical practice took longer than he had originally planned. He and Richard had gone over every patient's record, since they would be transferring to Richard's care. He wasn't able to persuade Marty to move to Bowersville, although she did say she would think about it. She was one of the best R.N.'s he had ever worked with, and he would have liked her assistance in Bowersville.

Arranging for his belongings to be packed and moved took only a phone call. The transfer of his medical equipment was a little more complicated. The disposal of his condo was left in the hands of a competent realtor. Since he didn't have any particular attachment to any of his furnishings, he had no problem about selling them.

Even though everything was going fairly smoothly, the one thing that had him chafing to get back to Bowersville was being unable to talk to Rachel. He had called her every night, but she hadn't answered at either her house or his aunt's. He even called her during the day, but didn't have any success then either. On the third day he phoned Mr. Grundy.

"You sure have trouble keeping track of your womenfolk, don't you, lad?" the irascible old man said.

"It seems so, Mr. Grundy. Would you happen to know where Rachel is? I haven't been able to get her on the phone for the last three days."

"That's cause she ain't there. She left on Friday."

"Left? What do you mean left?"

"Drove off in her car."

"Do you know where she went?"

"Nope. She does that sometimes. Doesn't say where she's going, but she always comes back."

Frustration and impatience were Thorn's constant

companions during the next two days and nights. Each night he phoned Mr. Grundy to see if Rachel had returned. Each night the elderly man told him no.

Finally on Tuesday evening Thorn arrived back in Bowersville. He drove by Rachel's house first. There were no lights in any of the windows, and her car was gone when he checked the garage.

Early the next morning a moving van pulled into the driveway of his aunt's house. By noon all his possessions had been unloaded under the supervision of Mr. Grundy and several other curious neighbors.

After the van departed, Thorn stood in the hall surrounded by boxes and crates, wondering where he should start first. A sharp tap on the frame of the open front door had him spinning around to see who it was. He had to swallow his disappointment when he saw Mr. Grundy instead of Rachel.

"Come in, Mr. Grundy. If you can."

His neighbor held up a brown bottle in one hand and two glasses in the other. "Thought you might need a pick-me-up, lad. Lord knows, I could do with one myself."

He poured several fingers of whiskey into the glasses and held one out to Thorn. Hiking himself up on one of the larger crates, he raised his glass and said, "Here's to your new home."

"Thanks." Thorn felt the whiskey burn his throat, then warm his stomach. He was going to have to keep Mr. Grundy's whiskey in mind if he ever needed an anesthetic. "Do you know of anyone who could do some carpentry work? There are a few changes that need to be made to convert part of the downstairs into an office and examining rooms."

Mr. Grundy let out his breath in a low whistle. "That's going to require a bit of doing, lad."

"I know, but it will be worth it."

Mr. Grundy hopped off the crate with the agility of a man much younger. "I'll make a few phone calls and get back to you." Tossing off the rest of the whiskey in one gulp, he added, "Thought you might be interested to know Rachel's red car was parked in front of Peabody's a little while ago. She should be home by now with her groceries."

Thorn slammed his glass down on a crate. "Why didn't you say so earlier?"

Mr. Grundy chuckled. "And ruin a good excuse for a glass of whiskey. Not on your life." Picking up the bottle, he strolled toward the door. "I'll take care of getting your carpenters. You tend to your lady."

Thorn didn't even bother to close his front door. He ran to his car and gunned it down the drive. It took only two minutes for him to drive to Rachel's and park behind her car.

He found her in the kitchen, putting groceries away, her back to him. She was wearing a suit and heels, the sleeves of the cobalt-blue jacket pushed up to her elbows. Her white silk blouse was unadorned by a collar or jewelry. She looked elegantly sophisticated and completely out of place in the country kitchen.

"Where in hell have you been?" he demanded.

Startled, she dropped a sack of apples as she whirled around. Placing her hand on her heart, she gasped, "You scared me."

He walked over to her, stepping around the apples littering the floor, and gripped her shoulders. He felt a flash of anger when he saw the shutters of wariness back in her eyes. He thought they had been removed for good, but there they were, effectively shutting him out.

He repeated his question, keeping an iron control on his anger and frustration. "Where have you been?"

"I went to New York."

"Why?"

"Business."

Her one-word reply was like a slap in the face. "Dammit! You're doing it again. I thought we were past this. You're closing yourself off from me again as though whatever you do is none of my business." His fingers tightened painfully on the fine bones of her shoulders. "Well, you're wrong. Why didn't you let me know you were going? I was worried about you."

Feeling defensive and hating it, she said, "How was I supposed to do that? I didn't know how to reach you in Des Moines."

"Well, that won't be a problem in the future." His hands skimmed down her back to her hips. "Next time I have to go out of town, you'll be coming with me. Next time you need to go to New York, I'll go with you. These last five days have been hell without you." His hands came up to frame her face. "I missed you, Rachel. I knew I would, but I didn't expect I would miss you as much as I did. It felt as if I'd been cut apart with a jagged knife."

He lowered his head and let his lips leave a trail of light, heated kisses over her neck and face. "Especially the nights. The long, lonely nights when I wanted you lying beside me or under me."

Rachel sighed his name and became lost in the depths of his eyes. She was mesmerized by how warm blue eyes could be when aroused. Her own eyes closed slowly as he claimed her mouth. His demanding kiss took her breath and sent frissons of heat rushing through her. Her teeth scraped along his tongue, and she reveled in the raw moan coming from deep in his throat.

His arms wrapped her in sensual magic as they fell into the chasm of mutual desire. Even though they had made love before, there was a different quality in each stroke, each caress, this time. The distance caused by the five-day separation had to be eliminated. The world became centered in each other, spinning and whirling with the growing demands of their passion.

There were still things to work out between them, but for now their physical needs overcame all others. Like a flash fire in dry grass, their desire burst into an uncontrollable blaze that could only be quenched in each other's arms.

Nine

Neither had eaten all day, and for once Rachel did justice to the meal they prepared together. Thorn sighed as he pushed his empty plate aside.

"This isn't getting those crates and boxes unpacked," he said.

Rachel had been adjusting the front opening of her satin robe but stopped to look up at him. "What crates and boxes?"

"Medical supplies, some things from my apartment. The movers dumped everything in the front hall, and that's where the medical equipment is going to have to stay until the renovations are done."

"Crates, boxes, movers, renovations. Thorn, what are you talking about?"

He leaned his arms on the table. He was clearly puzzled by her lack of comprehension. "I need the medical equipment for my practice." She was staring at him as though he had lost his mind. "What did you think I was talking about?"

"How would I know? For someone who's so adamant about communication, you're pretty close-mouthed. I didn't know you were thinking of moving your practice to Bowersville."

She, of course, knew the word flummoxed, but had never seen it before. It was the only way to describe the expression on his face.

He reached over and took her hand. "You're absolutely right. I guess I took it for granted you knew what I was doing. I discussed setting up a medical office in her house with Aunt Edith when I called her in Hawaii, but apparently I never told you." He lifted her hand to his mouth, touching her palm with his lips in a gesture of apology. "I'm sorry, Rachel. The only excuse I have for not telling you my plans is I usually have other things on my mind when I'm with you."

It was her turn to look dumbfounded. "You're moving here for good?"

"Of course. How else could we be together?"

She continued to stare at him. Several times she opened her mouth to speak, then clamped it shut. Finally she managed to put more than two words together with some sort of coherency. "Tell me now."

"Mr. Grundy is arranging for a carpenter to divide the rooms downstairs, converting the living room and dining room into examining rooms and an office. If I find I need more space later, I might build a small clinic. But for now I'm going to try to work out of the house like my father did when he started his family practice. I tried to convince one of our office nurses to move here, but Marty said she would have to think about it. Maybe I can get an R.N. from Algona. Where was I?"

He didn't wait for an answer, which was just as well because speech was beyond Rachel's capabilities at the moment. "There will be plenty of room upstairs for living quarters. Or we can live here if you'd rather." He smiled. "We will have to get some furniture though. We can't spend all our time in the kitchen and the bedroom. On second thought, forget the furniture. We don't even need to use the kitchen. We can live on love."

All the color drained from her face. She had just recovered from one shock when he dealt her another. She jerked her hand out of his, and her chair scraped against the floor as she pushed it away from the table and stood up.

"You're going too fast for me." Anger cut through her bewilderment, and she paced the floor several times, stopping in front of him with her hands on her hips. "You have a hell of a nerve, Thorn Cannon."

"True," he said complacently. "But why are you so upset about it? It can't come as any great shock after all this time."

"You nag me about being more trusting, more open about myself, and I've really tried. It hasn't been easy, but I've told you more about myself than I've ever told anyone else. Now you calmly announce you've made plans to move your practice to Bowersville and take it for granted I'm going to live with you. If, and right now it's a big if, if we live together, I would like to be consulted about it before you move in."

He stood up and framed her face with his hands, his fingers threading through her hair. "We will live together, Rachel. Married people usually do."

He didn't think she could have gotten any more

pale than she was. He was wrong. Her lips moved, mouthing the word 'married' without any sound.

His thumbs stroked and soothed. "I love you, Rachel. I want to marry you, have children with you, and live happily ever after with you. Maybe I haven't been fair to you, by not telling you sooner." He saw the expression in her eyes change and added, "All right, there's no maybe about it. I haven't been fair to you. I've treated you with all the finesse of a steamroller, but, dammit, you're just so damn elusive and self-contained, I didn't want to take a chance you wouldn't go along with what I had planned if you had time to think about it."

Rachel didn't realize she had been holding her breath until she felt a constricted pain in her chest. She sighed heavily, releasing the grip she had on his shirtfront. Her fingers felt cramped as she relaxed them and spread them out on his chest.

"I never dreamed you loved me," she said breathlessly. "It was too much to hope for, so I didn't expect it."

He pulled her closer. "I need to know how you feel, Rachel. I've taken a lot for granted between us, but this time I'm asking. Do you love me?"

The intent expression in his eyes wouldn't let her look away or deny her feelings. "Yes, I love you. You're the most arrogant man I've ever known. You drive me crazy half the time, when I'm with you and when I'm not, but I do love you."

He drew her into his arms, and she felt the tension flow out of his body, giving her an indication how important her answer had been to him. For a long time he simply held her, binding them together with the strength of his hold on her.

When he kissed her, his mouth communicated his feelings with a tenderness unlike anything she had ever experienced so fully before. Knowing she was loved gave her the confidence to completely release her own emotions.

His hands flowed over her back and hips, sliding the satin robe over the bare flesh underneath. The friction of the cool material against her warm skin incited a riot in his bloodstream. Maybe a lifetime would be long enough to fill himself with the pleasure of having her in his arms. He was complete only when she was near. And she loved him.

The sash of her robe loosened under his questing fingers. He slid his hands through the opening, seeking the warmth of her as he lowered his head to take her mouth. He held back his fierce desire to take her right there, trying to give her time to catch up to the passion searing his body.

When he felt her fingers on the snap of his jeans and heard the soft, yearning sounds from her throat, his control snapped.

The robe fell to the floor. His hand slipped between them to help her unfasten his jeans before he sank down on the chair behind him. His eyes locked with hers as he guided her hips over him, seeing ecstasy fill her as they were joined.

"You make me forget my name," he groaned as she began to move over him.

Pleasure shattered around them like tiny starbursts, blinding them to everything but each other.

The carpenter Mr. Grundy recommended estimated it would take him three weeks to do the renovations, including fresh paint and wallpaper. Thorn gladly left the choice of wallpaper to Rachel. Mr. Doyle, the expert with the hammer and saw, had some helpful suggestions about planning out the downstairs rooms, which were better than the ideas Thorn had had originally. Thorn gave him free rein, although he checked on the progress every day.

In the beginning Thorn was a little concerned when Mr. Doyle began to knock down walls. Gradually, out of the plaster dust and rubble, the individual rooms took shape. Rachel accompanied Thorn to Algona, where she helped him choose furniture for the waiting room and for his office. The bulk of Edith's furniture had been taken over to Rachel's house, where there was certainly enough room for it.

While Rachel worked on her comic strip during the day, Thorn sorted through his equipment, interviewed several women for the job of receptionist, and occasionally helped Mr. Doyle. The carpenter didn't trust Thorn to do much of the actual work since his skills with a hammer left a lot to be desired. He was allowed to fetch and carry and hold boards in position when the need arose.

On Sunday Rachel and Thorn were measuring the windows for curtains when they had a surprise visitor. Thorn almost fell off the ladder when he heard a familiar voice call out his name.

"Richard?"

The reply came from the front of the house. "In person. Where the hell are you?"

Thorn scrambled down the ladder. Raising his voice, he answered, "In here. Second door on your left."

They could hear several muttered complaints as Thorn's partner worked his way through the crowded hallway. Finally Richard made it to the doorway. He was a big man, a few inches shorter than Thorn, with wide shoulders and a thick neck. His build was the type football coaches drooled over when they were looking for someone to block six opponents. The one feature detracting from the image of an athletic Sherman tank was a pair of black horn-rimmed glasses he wore over sharp, intelligent brown eyes.

His smile was as broad as his physique. "Your patients could injure themselves just trying to get into your office."

Thorn clasped his hand. "That's only temporary. It's not that I'm not delighted to see you, but I can't help wondering who's minding the patients?"

"Olander owed me a favor," Richard said, naming a fellow physician. "I wanted to come to see what the attraction was that pulled you away from our lucrative clinic." His gaze shifted to Rachel. "I can't say that I blame you."

Thorn introduced them. "Rachel, I'd like you to meet my ex-partner, Richard Somerset. Richard, it's time you met the woman who will shortly be my wife, Rachel Hyatt."

Rachel watched the other man's reaction carefully for any signs of astonishment, but didn't find any. Instead, she was hauled toward him by his strong, huge hands on her shoulders and kissed resoundingly.

After raising his head, he looked down at her, a puzzled expression in his eyes. "You look vaguely familiar. Have I ever met you before other than in my dreams?"

She smiled, shaking her head. "I don't think so. I believe I would have remembered meeting a man who's bigger than my car."

His laughter showed his appreciation for her quick comeback. Then he grinned at Thorn. "Congratulations. You probably don't deserve her, but you always were a lucky devil."

Thorn smiled. "How long can you stay?"

Richard looked expectantly at Rachel. "I can stay for dinner."

Rachel smiled again. It was something she imagined people did automatically when they met Richard Somerset. "Consider yourself invited." Turning to Thorn, she added, "Why don't you show Richard around while I go to Peabody's?"

Thorn nodded, then put his hand behind her neck to bring her to him for a brief kiss. "We can just throw him some raw meat and he'll be content."

Both men watched Rachel leave the room, Richard with the same intent look. "I can understand why you were willing to chuck everything, old buddy," he said. "She's beautiful. I can't help feeling I've seen her somewhere before though. There's something familiar about her, but I can't pin it down."

"She's like no other woman in the world," Thorn said, completely serious.

"Dear Lord," Richard exclaimed. "The man is indeed smitten." His gaze roamed around the room. "Show me around. I'll be happy to give you the benefit of my vast experience. Then after I've worked up an appetite, we'll get back to your lovely lady." He suddenly had a look of horror on his face. "We aren't going to eat here, are we?"

Laughing, Thorn shook his head. "We'll go to Rachel's. Don't worry. We are fairly civilized here in Bowersville. We even use knives and forks. Let me show you the examining rooms first."

Dinner was a riotous affair. Richard had an interesting array of stories about patients, his football experiences, and some of the trials and tribulations he had undergone in medical school. The man also ate as though he hadn't seen food in days or this was to be his last meal for a very long time. Rachel had managed to buy three large Porterhouse steaks at Peabody's, thinking they would be more than enough to eat, along with a salad and baked potatoes.

Richard not only ate every bite of his steak, but also had an unusual penchant for reaching across the table to stick his fork in whatever took his fancy on anyone else's plate. The first time he swiped a bite of steak off Thorn's plate, Rachel noticed Thorn acted as though it was perfectly normal. Apparently it was. When Richard casually speared a cherry tomato out of her salad, she copied Thorn's attitude of indifference.

During the meal Rachel was aware of the occasional searching glances she received from Richard. She didn't know if his attention was from curiosity because of Thorn's involvement with her, or for some other reason. She didn't get the impression there was anything personal in the way he stared at her. He wasn't attracted to her, she decided, just extremely curious.

As they lingered over coffee, Richard said bluntly to Rachel, "When Thorn told me he was ending our partnership to move to a dinky town I never even heard of and set up a family practice, I thought he was nuts. I thought he would be wasting his talents as a doctor, not to mention giving up a sizable income." He leaned back in his chair. "That's why I had to come and see for myself."

"Were you going to try to talk him out of it?" she asked.

His smile was faintly mocking. "Maybe. But then I saw the two of you together and met a couple of people who came to the house while I was looking around. From what they said, I gather there is a *definite* need for a doctor in this town. They seemed extremely grateful Thorn was settling here."

Rachel glanced at Thorn, but before she could pose the question, he answered it. "Marne brought her husband and the baby to the house. He wanted to thank me for delivering the baby." He grinned. "Mr. Grundy dropped by too."

Richard shook his head. "He gave me a sack of popcorn to take back to Des Moines. It's still on the cob."

"Do you still think Thorn is making a mistake?" Rachel asked.

"Maybe this is what it's all about," Richard said. "Home, heart, and health. Which reminds me. When's the wedding?"

"In two weeks," Thorn answered easily. Ignoring Rachel's sudden intake of breath, he asked, "Think you can make it? I'd like you to be my best man."

"I wouldn't miss it. I have to make sure you're officially out of circulation." Whether it was because he saw the expression on Rachel's face or because he wanted to get on the road, he abruptly pushed back his chair. "I hate to eat and run, but I'd better hit the road. Thanks for the great meal, Rachel, and

I'm glad I finally got to meet you. I didn't believe Thorn when he talked about you last week. Now I know he was telling the truth."

Since Rachel didn't know what Thorn had said, she didn't comment other than to say she was pleased to meet him too. While Thorn walked his friend out to his car, she went into the living room, filled now with Edith's furniture. She sat on the couch and thought about Thorn telling Richard the wedding would be in two weeks. By the time he returned to the house, she had a choice selection of things to say.

He sat down beside her and sighed heavily. "Okay, let me have it."

She did exactly that. "Why did you tell Richard we were going to be married in two weeks?"

"Because it's true."

"Don't you think that's something we both should decide?"

"Probably."

"So why did you announce it like that without discussing it with me first?"

She gasped in surprise when he lifted her easily onto his lap. Keeping one arm around her, he rested the other across her thighs. "I'm tired of all this sneaking around and spending every night alone for the sake of the neighbors. I want to get started on our life together, Rachel."

Leaning against his chest, she was aware of the scent and heat of him dissolving her frustrated anger. "I'm just getting used to the fact you love me. I haven't had time to think about marrying you."

"Well, take the time now."

She slid her arm around his neck. "Thorn, maybe

we should wait a while longer, get to know each other better. We're so different. You're an extrovert and I'm an introvert. You have a lot of adjusting to do with starting a new practice and moving into a small town. Don't you think that's enough to adapt to all at once without throwing in a wife?"

His hand slowly stroked her shapely thigh. "I know everything I need to know about you. I love you, and I can't imagine living my life without you."

Her eyes seemed bigger and darker in the reflected moonlight. Was she trying to back out of making a final commitment to him, he wondered. If she was, she was going to be disappointed.

He kissed her. "I can adjust to anything but doing without you."

She had tried. Her other arm encircled his neck. "I hope you know what you're doing. I would hate it if the day came when you regretted marrying me."

The knot of tension began to loosen in his stomach. His hand slid up her hip to her breast, and his thumb caressed the tantalizing hard bud through the material of her shirt. "I know exactly what I'm doing. If you need to be shown, I'll be happy to oblige."

She arched her back to bring her breast more fully into his hand. "Is this how you're going to get out of discussing things with me? You know I can't think when you touch me like that."

His lips caressed the sweet flesh of her neck. "Do you want to marry me?"

Her answer came out in a breathless rush when his teeth nipped gently at a sensitive spot below her ear. "Yes."

"I want a preacher, not a justice of the peace, no

offense, but a real preacher, a church, and the whole town invited. I just might be able to wait two weeks, but I can't guarantee any longer."

"That doesn't give me much time."

His voice was lazy, low, and husky as he enjoyed the taste of her warm skin. "For what?"

She chuckled. "Honestly, Thorn. You think all you have to do is say we're getting married and everything will automatically fall into place. I hate to sound like a cliché, but I don't have anything to wear to a wedding."

With deft fingers he opened the front of her shirt. "You look gorgeous in whatever you wear. If you want a wedding dress, go buy one. There's bound to be something in Algona or Des Moines." He softly kissed her breast. "If you need to fly to New York in order to find what you want, I'll go with you."

"You won't have time. You're opening up your medical practice in a couple of days, remember?"

As far as he was concerned, the matter of what she would wear was settled. There was one other thing he wanted to mention though. Holding her away from him so he could see her face, he said, "One disadvantage in having a small practice is I'm not going to have a partner to take over when I want some free time. Is that going to be a problem for you?"

"I don't see why there would be any problems. I have my own work to do."

His hand stroked across her rib cage to fasten on to her breast. "Are we through talking? I can think of other things I'd rather do right now."

"This is why we never get around to discussing things."

He smiled. "There are different ways to communicate than talking."

And he began to show her one of them.

Thorn took care of making the arrangements with the church for the wedding. The news flew through the town shortly after he left the parsonage. Several ladies from the church marched up to Rachel's front door, volunteering to supply the food for the reception. Their generosity was one of the things Rachel liked about the small town. When she had first moved to Bowersville, people had made her feel welcome even though she wasn't particularly receptive to their friendly overtures. Now she realized she was one of them, in her heart and in her mind. She invited them in and served them coffee while they discussed what they would like to serve.

The renovations were almost finished and Thorn was in his new office when he received a phone call from Richard. He had been about to go to Rachel's but was happy to talk to his ex-partner.

A few minutes later he set the phone back down with extra care. What he really wanted to do was throw the damn thing across the room. Instead of leaving as he had planned, he sat down behind his new desk. He had some thinking to do before he saw Rachel again.

An hour later he entered Rachel's, the house he would be living in with her in less than two weeks. An inviting fragrance filled the air, letting him know she had started dinner. He didn't find her in the kitchen, however. She was in her studio.

Rachel had her earphones on and didn't hear Thorn's footsteps on the hardwood floor. Bent over her drawing board, a pen in her hand, she didn't know anyone was there until her music suddenly stopped. She glanced over at the Walkman resting on a table and saw Thorn's hand on the control.

Smiling, she reached up to remove the earphones, "Hi. I didn't know you were home." Her smile faded when she saw the hard expression in his eyes. "What's wrong?"

"Why didn't you ever tell me you were a model?"

Ten

Rachel wondered why he seemed so angry. "Does it matter that I was once a model?"

"It does when I didn't know about it. I felt like a fool when Richard called and gave me a hard time because I hadn't told him about your modeling career. I told him he was nuts and imagine my surprise when he said he had a magazine in front of him with a picture of you on the cover. Ever since he met you he had the nagging feeling he had seen you somewhere before, but he couldn't think of where until he was walking through the waiting room of the clinic. On top of a stack of old magazines was one with your picture on the cover. It was about two years old and you were dressed in an evening gown, but he recognized you."

Rachel got off the stool and moved away from the drawing table. "I thought you said you knew everything you needed to know about me."

"I was wrong. Why didn't you ever tell me about

your previous career? It makes me wonder if you would have kept 'Fancie Fanny' from me if I hadn't come barging in here."

"You are wrong again. I would have told you about the comic strip once we became—"

"Lovers? Otherwise you wouldn't have mentioned Fannie at all, would you?"

"Once we became involved," she corrected him.

"Then why didn't you tell me about your modeling? I'm not exactly a stranger. It would be something I'd be interested in." His eyes narrowed. "Or did you pose for some other types of pictures that wouldn't be classed as 'fasionable'?"

The implication hit her like a physical blow. Her color faded. "I did only straightforward modeling for fashion layouts and occasionally did runway work. I never did any type of nudity if that's what you're implying."

He strode across the room, his anger making him restless. Then he whirled to face her.

"One thing that puzzled me when I first saw you in the river was your lack of modesty, yet you were uncomfortable when I touched you. I could never understand how you could feel so free about dressing in front of me, but flinched when I came too close." There was a hard edge to his voice when he added, "Now I understand. You're used to dressing and undressing in front of other people."

"You make it sound as though I was involved in something unsavory. You should know me better than that."

"I'm not sure I know you at all. I thought we had gotten past keeping secrets from each other. If your modeling was so respectable, why haven't you ever told me about it?"

Feeling suddenly chilled, she wrapped her arms around her waist and walked over to one of the windows. Staring outside, she said quietly, "I honestly didn't think it was that important. The years I spent modeling in New York are not my fondest memories. I hated every minute spent changing from one outfit to another and standing under hot lights in front of a camera."

"Then why did you do it?"

He saw her shoulders move stiffly as she shrugged. "When I graduated from high school, my grandfather considered me to be on my own. I had no formal training of any kind, so when a girl I had known in school suggested I go with her to an agency, I did. I had to do something. I was a lousy waitress and not much better as a clerk in a department store. I needed to earn money somehow, and modeling seemed a fairly easy way to do it while I studied drawing at night."

"I suppose there are worse ways of making a living," he conceded, although he still didn't like the idea of her parading around in front of people or posing for a camera in various stages of undress. What he disliked even more was that he had had to hear about her past from someone else instead of from her.

"Why did you stop modeling?"

"I no longer needed the income. It had served its purpose. Besides, changing clothes twenty times a day began to lose its appeal after a while. Sometimes clothespins and straight pins were used to make an outfit fit better. Once I was sewn into a dress because the zipper was broken and there wasn't time to fix it. All that ever mattered was that I looked good, the clothes looked good. After a while none of that seemed very important to me. The creator of a comic strip might not rate all that high in some other people's viewpoint, but I never got the sense of accomplishment out of modeling that I get from creating the comic strip."

At that moment the phone rang. Rachel continued looking out the window. Thorn stepped over to the table where the telephone was and answered it.

A few minutes later he hung up after telling whoever it was that he would be right there.

"I have to go. That was Marne. She wants me to come out to check the baby. He's got a cough and she's worried about him. I'll be back as soon as I can. Then we'll talk."

He didn't give her a chance to say anything. He simply turned and left.

Rachel didn't move from her position by the window for a long time. Then she left the studio and walked into the kitchen. She opened a drawer, took out her notebook, and turned a number of pages until she found what she wanted. Taking the notebook with her, she walked over to the phone and punched out eleven numbers.

Her call was answered after the first ring.

"Hello, Henry," she said. "I'm sorry to bother you at home, but I have a big favor to ask."

The first indication Thorn had that Rachel had left town was when he stopped in to check on Mrs. Lindstrom. She told him her husband had seen Rachel's red car leaving town when he returned from Algona.

Somehow Thorn finished his examination of Mrs. Lindstrom, telling her she could return to the café as long as she took it easy and didn't overdo. Then he drove immediately to Rachel's house. Mrs. Lindstrom had been right. Rachel's car was gone, and after checking the house completely from basement to attic, he didn't find a note telling him where she had gone.

He paced back and forth restlessly, cursing himself for not staying and settling their earlier disagreement. Looking back, he realized he hadn't made it clear he didn't object to her having been a model, only that she hadn't told him about it. He'd been pigheaded and dictatorial, acting like a super macho jerk. It wasn't too surprising she hadn't liked it.

On impulse he went to the kitchen to look for her notebook, but it was gone. Without it he had no way of knowing where to look for her or how to contact her agent. There were few other people he could think of who might know where she would go.

He slammed his fist against a wall. He had pushed too hard too soon.

He sat up all night waiting for her, but she didn't return. The following day he finished arranging his medical office in between futile phone calls to Rachel's. That evening he camped out again at her house, this time on her bed, although he got little sleep.

As each minute passed without her, the more worried and helpless he felt.

The next day he showed his new receptionist/secretary around the office. Doris Jackson was a woman in her forties who had worked in an insurance office in Algona, so she was familiar with the usual medical forms. He was lucky to find her. Actually she had found him, appearing on his doorstep to apply for the job. She didn't like driving to and from Algona every day, especially in the winter.

She was a friendly, caring woman who wasn't afraid to take over all the paperwork and answering the phone. She was also willing to act as assistant until he could hire a nurse.

Leaving her to set up her desk and an appointment system, he saw a couple of patients. With all he had to do, he never stopped thinking about Rachel. He kept telling himself she had to come back to Bowersville sometime. He had to believe that.

After Mrs. Jackson was gone for the day, he was about to leave his office to continue his vigil at Rachel's when Mr. Grundy walked in.

"Hello, lad. I'm glad I caught you before you left. I was hoping you would come over and have dinner with me tonight."

"I don't think I would be very good company, Mr. Grundy."

"Nonsense."

"I'm a fool, Mr. Grundy."

"Most men are when it comes to love." Mr. Grundy took Thorn's arm and steered him toward the door. "Trust an old man to know how to cheer up a young man in love. We'll have dinner and a couple of drinks while I tell you how to handle women. You youngsters don't know how to manage things, that's for certain."

Thorn wasn't wild about the whole town knowing he and Rachel were having problems, but there wasn't much he could do about it. The prospect of spending the evening alone had him accompanying Mr.

Grundy next door. What the hell, he thought as he crossed the lawn with Mr. Grundy. Maybe he'd learn something. Lord knew he wasn't managing too well on his own.

Three hours later he said good night to Mr. Grundy and slowly walked back to his aunt's house. As tired as he was, he was glad he hadn't had more than one drink of his neighbor's brandy. In fact, he was so exhausted, he was going to take Mr. Grundy's advice and stay at his aunt's instead of going to Rachel's.

Once inside, he locked the door and started up the stairs. He began to unbutton his shirt, pulling it out of his slacks as he pushed open the door to his attic bedroom. With his elbow he flicked the light switch by the door. He stopped.

His room had been transformed. Every inch of the walls beside and behind his bed were plastered floor to ceiling with glossy black and white and color photos of Rachel. There were over a hundred of them. He slowly walked closer to examine them. Her beauty stood out and hit him in the gut.

He was about to sit on his bed when he noticed there was a cardboard box in the middle of it. He sat down and pulled the box over to him. Opening it up, he looked inside. The first thing he took out was a copy of a birth certificate for Rachel Dorsey Hyatt. Then he removed a rubber band from around a stack of report cards. He examined every single one, reading the comments of her teachers and looking at her grades. He lifted the lid of a shoebox and took out some photographs of a much younger Rachel dressed in a school uniform standing with other girls also in uniform. There were none of her that might have been taken in Bowersville. Nor were there any pictures of her grandfather or parents.

A file folder was under the shoebox. Inside were medical records, including a small booklet that contained a list of the innoculations she had received over the years.

It took Thorn over an hour to wade through every scrap of paper in the box. Then he got off the bed to study the photos once again.

Rachel paced up and down in front of the glass wall of her studio. She was too restless even to attempt to work. It had been over an hour since Mr. Grundy had phoned her, telling her Thorn had returned to Edith's house. Using Mr. Grundy as an accomplice had been the only way she could insure Thorn wouldn't be in Edith's house for a while, and it was obvious Mr. Grundy had enjoyed his role as cupid.

After telling her Thorn had left, he'd said, "That lad feels lower than a snail's belly. Take it easy on him."

Continuing her pacing, she glanced at her watch. He had had plenty of time to look through all the stuff she had left in his bedroom. She stopped abruptly. Unless he hadn't gone to his bedroom. Maybe she should have left everything in his office, or even in the front hall.

Of course there was also the possibility he had swept everything aside and gone to sleep. Mr. Grundy had said he was tired and cranky.

She might as well go to bed herself, although she didn't expect to sleep any better than she had the previous two nights. It looked as if she was going to have to try the direct approach. But not tonight.

Halfway up the stairs she paused on a step. She was either imagining things or there was an unusual scent in the air. It wasn't like her perfume. The fragrance was sweet and flowery rather than spicy. With her hand on the rail she slowly continued up the stairs. Her bedroom door was ajar by several inches, and she could see a soft yellow glow lighting the room.

Her heartbeat accelerated until she could hear her pulse beating in her ears. Her reaction wasn't from fear, but from anticipation.

Placing her palm against the door, she pushed it open farther and entered the room. Disappointment hit her a hard blow when she glanced around the bedroom and found it empty. She had expected and hoped Thorn would be there, but her room looked the same as usual.

Except for a lighted candle beside her bed and six yellow roses resting in a cluster on her pillow. She recognized the roses. They were from Edith's garden. When she leaned over and picked up one of the fragrant flowers, she noticed a white piece of paper underneath them.

She picked it up and unfolded it. Written in black bold print, was:

YOUR PRESENCE IS REQUESTED FOR THE GRAND OPENING OF RACHEL'S TREEHOUSE. SECOND OAK TREE ON THE RIGHT. DRESS CASUAL.

Just to be on the safe side, she read the note several times. Then, her heart in her throat, she picked up the candle and left the room.

The sound of crickets filled the night air. The

grass was cool and damp with dew as she walked in her bare feet to the large oak tree in the corner of the backyard. Its leaves and the darkness made it too difficult for her to see anything beyond the glow from her candle.

She stopped near the trunk of the tree and looked up. All she could see was a dark mass where the tree branched off in three different directions. Then the light from the candle shone on another piece of paper attached to a dangling rope.

Holding the candle closer to the paper, she read, PULL.

She gave the rope a yank and heard the tinkling of a bell. Looking up, she saw a sliver of light gradually broaden as a trapdoor was lifted. A rope ladder was dropped through the opening, unrolling swiftly as it descended in front of her. She blew out the candle and set it on the ground, then grasped the rope and began to climb. The light grew brighter with each step she took.

As her head and shoulders appeared through the opening, two strong, familiar hands grasped her shoulders and pulled her through. She knelt on the floor as Thorn shut the trapdoor, then he reached for her.

He took her mouth with a desperation born out of the frustration and worry of the last couple of days without her. He needed to know how she felt about him, whether she had changed her mind, and this was one way of finding out. He got his answer as she responded hungrily.

The tension drained out of his body. As badly as he wanted her, would always want her, he drew away from her. "No. This time we talk first."

She knew he was right. They did have a lot to discuss. Sitting back on her heels, she glanced around. Several candles and a lantern placed in the corners of the eight-foot-square tree house gave off enough light for her to see clearly. The floor and walls were all done in smooth pine lumber. Two small windows were set opposite each other, with dark material tacked over them so light wouldn't show from the outside.

Turning back to Thorn, she asked, "When did you do all this?"

"I didn't. Mr. Doyle did."

"When?"

"The day before yesterday. When I found out you had left town, I asked Mr. Doyle to build this tree house for you as a surprise for when you got back. It took him only one day."

"Why? Why did you want him to build the tree house?"

He grimaced. "I don't know. Maybe I was grasping at straws, thinking that if I had the tree house built, it would give you something to come home for. It seemed like a good idea at the time. Now it sounds like I've lost my marbles."

"I think it's sweet, but you didn't have to go to all that trouble. I was coming back."

He raised his hand and touched her face, as though he needed to make sure it was really she and not a dream. "Why did you leave? I've been going crazy wondering where you were, if you were all right."

"I stayed in a motel in Algona to wait for some things to arrive from New York. It took a while for Henry to gather up all the pictures I wanted. Even sending them by overnight mail, he couldn't get everything I needed right away. Besides, I needed the time alone to think."

His finger stroked her jaw. "Rachel, I'm sorry. I was wrong to think you didn't trust me by not telling me about your career in modeling. You trusted me enough to love me. I should have realized I didn't need more than that."

"I've had a lot of time to think the last couple of days. I should have realized why it was so important for you to know about my past. Your medical training makes you want to know all the facts in order to make a proper diagnosis. That's just the way you are. I thought about when you were examining Mrs. Lindstrom and when you talked to Marne before the baby was born. You needed to gather as many facts as you could before you could feel comfortable with your medical decision. I should have understood that. Just as you have to understand the way I am. I might not always tell you how I feel, but that doesn't mean I don't feel."

Thorn dropped his hand. "You have to stop taking off like you do, Rachel. You're going to put me in an early grave."

"I promise. And you have to promise to talk things over with me instead of charging ahead without me. I admit I'm new at this communication stuff you rant and rave about, but it seems to me it's supposed to work both ways."

He put his arms around her. "I'm sorry, Rachel. For the misunderstandings, for the last couple of days, for being a pigheaded idiot. I can't promise to change overnight, but I promise to try to include you in every aspect of my life from now on." He lowered his head, pressing his mouth to her throat.

His voice was low and hoarse. "Our life together might be full of hills and valleys, but it certainly won't be dull."

She let her weight rest against him, her arms sliding up around his neck. "With you building tree houses and delivering babies, it's certainly going to be interesting. Just out of curiosity, what did you tell Mr. Doyle when you asked him to build this tree house?"

"I told him I wanted it for our children. He agreed to do it, but he gave me a strange look."

"No wonder, considering we aren't even married yet, much less expecting a child."

Thorn's hand slid down to her stomach. "Someday I want to feel our child move inside you."

She trembled at his touch. "This is one of the things we need to discuss. I want two. A boy and a girl."

His hand moved lower. "I thought we would have four. Two boys and two girls."

Her lips caressed his throat. "We'll compromise. Three. Assorted."

His deep chuckle vibrated through her as he kissed her, lowering her to the floor of the tree house. "We'll discuss it." His lips touched hers lightly, then harder. "Later."

THE EDITOR'S CORNER

Get ready for a month chockfull of adventure and romance! In October our LOVESWEPT heroes are a bold and dashing group, and you'll envy the heroines who win their hearts.

Starting off the month, we have **HOT TOUCH,** LOVE-SWEPT #354. Deborah Smith brings to life a dreamy hero in rugged vet Paul Belue. When Caroline Fitzsimmons arrives at Paul's bayou mansion to train his pet wolf for a movie, she wishes she could tame the male of her species the way she works her magic with animals. The elegant and mysterious Caroline fascinates Paul and makes him burn for her caresses, and when he whispers "Chere" in his Cajun drawl, he melts her resistance. A unique and utterly sensual romance, **HOT TOUCH** sizzles!

Your enthusiastic response to Gail Douglas's work has thrilled us all and has set Gail's creative juices flowing. Her next offering is a quartet of books called *The Dreamweavers.* Hop onboard for your first romantic journey with Morgan Sinclair in LOVESWEPT #355, **SWASHBUCKLING LADY.** Morgan and her three sisters run The Dreamweavers, an innovative travel company. And you'll be along for the ride to places exotic as each falls in love with the man of her dreams.

When hero Cole Jameson spots alluring pirate queen Morgan, he thinks he's waltzed into an old Errol Flynn movie! But Morgan enjoys her role as Captain of a restored brigantine, and she plays it brilliantly for the tourists of Key West. In Morgan, Cole finds a woman who's totally guileless, totally without pretense—and he doesn't know how to react to her honesty, especially since he can't disclose his own reasons for being in Key West. Intrigued and infuriated by Cole's elusive nature, Morgan thinks she's sailing in unchar-

(continued)

tered waters. We guarantee you'll love these two charming characters—or we'll walk the plank!

One of our favorite writing teams, Adrienne Staff and Sally Goldenbaum return with **THE GREAT AMERICAN BACHELOR**, LOVESWEPT #356. Imagine you're on the worst blind date of your life . . . and then you're spirited away on a luxury yacht by a handsome hunk known in the tabloids as the Great American Bachelor! Cathy Stevenson is saved—literally—by Michael Winters when he pulls her from the ocean, and her nightmare turns into a romantic dream. Talk about envying a heroine! You'll definitely want to trade places with Cathy in this story of a modern day Robinson Crusoe and his lady love!

Peggy Webb will take you soaring beyond the stars with **HIGHER THAN EAGLES**, LOVESWEPT #357. From the first line you'll be drawn into this powerfully evocative romance.

A widow with a young son, Rachel Windham curses the fates who've brought the irresistible pilot Jacob Donovan back from his dangerous job of fighting oil rig fires. Jacob stalks her relentlessly, demanding she explain why she'd turned her back on him and fled into marriage to another man, and Rachel can't escape—not from the mistakes of the past, nor the yearning his mere presence stirs in her. Peggy does a superb job in leading Rachel and Jacob full circle through their hurts and disappointments to meet their destiny in each other's arms.

Next in our LOVESWEPT lineup is #358, **FAMILIAR WORDS** by Mary Kay McComas. Mary Kay creates vividly real characters in this sensitive love story between two single parents.

Beth Simms is mortified when her little boy, Scotty, calls ruggedly handsome Jack Reardan "daddy" during the middle of Sunday church services. She knows that every male Scotty sees is "daddy," but

(continued)

there's something different about this man whose wicked teasing makes her blush. Jack bulldozes Beth's defenses and forges a path straight to her heart. You won't want to miss this lively tale, it's peppered with humor and emotion as only Mary Kay can mix them!

Barbara Boswell finishes this dazzling month with **ONE STEP FROM PARADISE**, LOVESWEPT #359. Police officer Lianna Novak is furious when she's transferred to Burglary, but desire overwhelms her fury when she meets Detective Michael Kirvaly. Urged on by wild, dangerous feelings for Michael, Lianna risks everything by falling in love with her new partner. Michael's undeniable attraction to Lianna isn't standard operating procedure, but the minute the sultry firecracker with the sparkling eyes approached his desk, he knew he'd never let her go—even if he had to handcuff her to him and throw away the key. Barbara will really capture your heart with this delightful romance.

We're excited and curious to know what you think of our new look, so do write and tell us. We hope you enjoy it!

Best wishes from the entire LOVESWEPT staff,
Sincerely,

Carolyn Nichols

Carolyn Nichols
Editor
LOVESWEPT
Bantam Books
666 Fifth Avenue
New York, NY 10103

60 Minutes to a Better, More Beautiful You!

Now it's easier than ever to awaken your sensuality, stay slim forever—even make yourself irresistible. With Bantam's bestselling subliminal audio tapes, you're only 60 minutes away from a better, more beautiful you!

__ 45004-2	**Slim Forever**	....	$8.95
__ 45112-X	**Awaken Your Sensuality**	....	$7.95
__ 45081-6	**You're Irresistible**	....	$7.95
__ 45035-2	**Stop Smoking Forever**	....	$8.95
__ 45130-8	**Develop Your Intuition**	....	$7.95
__ 45022-0	**Positively Change Your Life**	...	$8.95
__ 45154-5	**Get What You Want**	....	$7.95
__ 45041-7	**Stress Free Forever**	....	$7.95
__ 45106-5	**Get a Good Night's Sleep**	....	$7.95
__ 45094-8	**Improve Your Concentration**	.	$7.95
__ 45172-3	**Develop A Perfect Memory**	.....	$8.95

Bantam Books, Dept. LT, 414 East Golf Road, Des Plaines, IL 60016

Please send me the items I have checked above. I am enclosing $_____ (please add $2.00 to cover postage and handling). Send check or money order, no cash or C.O.D.s please. (Tape offer good in USA only.)

Mr/Ms _____

Address _____

City/State_____ Zip_____

LT-8/89

Please allow four to six weeks for delivery. This offer expires 2/90. Prices and availability subject to change without notice.